The

SWORD

of the

SPIRIT:

The

SWORD
of the
SPIRIT:

In the Shadow of Death

WAYMAN JACKSON

XULON PRESS

Xulon Press
2301 Lucien Way #415
Maitland, FL 32751
407.339.4217
www.xulonpress.com

Paperback ISBN-13: 978-1-66283-514-8
eBook ISBN-13: 978-1-66283-515-5

OTHER BOOKS BY THE AUTHOR:

The sword of the Spirit: City on the brink

The sword of the Spirit: the full armor of God

ACKNOWLEDGMENTS

I want to thank the Lord Jesus Christ for the material needed to write this book.

TABLE OF CONTENTS

Prologue: Satan's Quest xi

1. Hidden Plot 1
2. The Ceremony 8
3. Breaking the Ice 11
4. The Proposal 15
5. Longing 20
6. Dead Ends 23
7. Help Mate 25
8. The Audition 28
9. One More Step 32
10. Final Step 35
11. Haunted House 38
12. Aftermath 44
13. Sleepless Night 47
14. The beginning of sorrows 51
15. The Bridal Store 53
16. Loyalty 58
17. Chance Encounter 62
18. Love Unrealized 66
19. Cold Feet 71
20. The Wedding 74
21. The Reception 79
22. The Reception: Part 2 83
23. Affection & Attraction 89
24. Keep the Faith 95
25. The Wait is over 99
26. Unknown Sickness 101

27. Medical Emergency 103
28. Hospital stay. 105
29. Love's cocoon & outside worries 107
30. Road trip. 110
31. The Coast 112
32. The City of Light 115
33. Downtown 121
34. Hidden Enemy. 124
35. Past plot 126
36. New Plot 131
37. A Revival, Maybe? 136
38. Hidden danger 141
39. Invisible enemy. 144
40. Revelation. 147
41. Professional "help" 151
42. Vote of no confidence. 156
43. The Invasion 158
44. Can we pray? 160
45. "I AM with you". 163
46. The exam 171
47. Opened Eyes 176
48. The Revival. 181
49. The free offer. 184
50. Eye of the storm. 187
51. Storm Surge 190
52. Unwelcomed guest 196
53. The Spirit Warrior 199
54. The Reunion. 205

PROLOGUE: SATAN'S QUEST

IN THE MIDDLE OF A MOONLIT SKY, ON A JETLINER, a famous singer, Alexia, and her band of performers lounge in first class. Yellow lighting of the cabin gives off a warm golden glow. However, in the essence of her soul lies shivering darkness. The cold darkness in her soul, a conscious choice of her own, compounds pressure in her mind.

Early in adolescence, having a dynamic voice and desiring fame and fortune, she ran away from home. With nothing keeping her there except to support her mother amid an alcoholic father, she took her dreams and ran away.

Walking down the street in the middle of a cold bustling city, a black limo with tinted windows pulls up next to her. Alexia stops and peers at the window, and it rolls down. A tan-skinned man with a chiseled face and chocolate brown hair and eyes stare into hers. Her heart flutters in her chest.

"Excuse me, miss," he says in a smooth voice. "I couldn't help but to stop and speak to you. You're very beautiful, and I couldn't see myself passing you by until I had a chance to say something."

"What's your name?" asks Alexia.

"Warlord."

"What kind of name is Warlord?" she says as butterflies flutter in her stomach.

"It's my stage name. You see, I'm a music producer." Alexia's eyes widen as she gasps. "I'm always looking for the next big thing, if you know what I mean." Alexia nods her head. "With a pretty face like yours, you would be the next hit in pop music," Warlord says with a tooth-filled grin.

"You really think so?"

"Of course." He opens the limo door. He's dressed in a black three-piece suit. The black suit is red pinstriped. Warlord extends his hand. "Just take a ride with me, and I can show you a world that you can only dream of."

Alexia reaches for his hand, and chills envelope her body. Her heart slows and becomes heavy. Thoughts of death fills her mind, and she pulls her hand back.

"I... I don't know."

"What's not to know? Aren't you out here in the big city searching for your dreams?"

"Yeah."

"Then this is a sign," he says with a smile. "It's not every day that a music producer stops someone on the side of the road handing them a chance at a contract. Am I right?"

"Yeah, but..."

"You know what? It's okay. Don't even worry about it." Warlord closes the door and motions for the driver to drive off.

"No, wait!"

Warlord turns his head. "Wait for what?"

"I want to come with you," she says.

"Okay." He opens the door and extends his hand. "Then take my hand."

She extends her hand. Cold sweat drips down her face, and her hand starts to quiver.

Anything is better than being on the street. I could die out here. At least he is giving me a chance at my dreams, Alexia thinks to herself as she takes hold of his hand and joins him in the limo.

Warlord takes Alexia to a fancy restaurant and reveals to her that he is an angel confined to earth. The type of angel he is he has kept secret until he pulls a necklace from out of his pocket. He hangs the necklace in the air, and it's a devil star necklace. It shines as it reflects the light from the candles.

"All you have to do is grab this star, make me your master, and I'll give you everything you ever dreamed of."

With fame and fortune glittering in her mind, Alexia snatches it from his hand. In a short time, she becomes a mega star. People obsess over her voice and beauty.

At first, Alexia enjoys the fame and fortune promised, but now, after the Spirit warrior, Hezekiah, destroyed Warlord in the battle for Central City, she is not so sure about her own life. The thought of death sends an icy shiver down her spine. Alexia glances out the window, and a black ghoul is on the wing!

"Miss, would you like some champagne?" asks the flight attendant.

"Yes," says Alexia. She puts her icy hand on her face. Alexia glances out the window, and the dark figure is gone. She flicks her crimson red hair from her eyes. Her tremoring hands reach for the crystal wine glass. The attendant pours the bubbling champagne in her glass. It swirls to the top. Alexia handles the glass and takes a sip. The bubbles swirl into her mouth and pop in her throat. Alexia leans into her seat, and the flight attendant turns to another passenger. Alexia glances out the window. The dark figure sits on the wing, staring at her. Its shiny red eyes pierce into her icy soul.

"Miss, would you like some more?" asks the flight attendant.

"Yes, just give me the whole bottle." She turns back to the window, and nothing's there. "I need to calm down."

She grabs the champagne bottle and chugs a gulp. The flight attendant turns to another passenger, and the plane quakes. Everyone pops from their seat. The flight attendant stumbles and grabs Alexia's seat. All luggage spills out onto the floor.

Conversation rumbles throughout the plane. The intercom sparks and squeaks. People cover their ears.

"Everyone, stay calm. We are experiencing a little turbulence," says the captain over the intercom.

The plane trembles, and people fall into the aisle. Alexia turns toward the window, and the dark figure is clawing into the wing!

"Everyone, please remain calm," says the captain as emergency equipment drops from the ceiling.

"Stop! Please stop!" shouts Alexia as her pulse pounds into her ears. The creature pauses, cocks its head toward her, and it turns its head back and hacks at the plane's wing. She takes out her devil star necklace and puts it against the window. The star shines in the moon light. The creature turns its head and rushes toward the window. Alexia gasps. It stops outside the window and peers at the shimmering star.

The creature scans her and nods its head. She turns away from the window, leans into the seat, and lays her head back. Alexia closes her eyes and exhales. The plane trembles and tilts and Alexia opens her eyes.

The flight attendant flies toward Alexia's window. Her face slams into the window, and her body contorts. The attendant lands in Alexia's lap, limp. Alexia screams and jumps out her seat, knocking the dead attendant to the floor. She glances back out the window. More dark creatures descend onto the aircraft's wing and claw into it! The black ghouls scrape through aluminum and wires as sparks fly around the dark beasts.

"Prepare for an emergency landing!" shouts the captain.

At sea? Alexia sprints down the aisle, looking for someone, anyone, who prays to God. The plane turns 360 degrees, and Alexia hits the ceiling and flies through the cabin. She hits a wall and slams into the deck, snapping her nose. As she gets up, blood runs from her nose, and with her heart thumping in her chest, she gazes at the wing. It's completely gone!

The plane plummets, and people scream. Alexia hears scraping steel above her. *Are they clawing through the plane?* The plane tumbles, and she hits the ceiling again. Centrifugal force holds Alexia prisoner on the ceiling.

She peers down and notices a woman and her little boy. The mother desperately holds onto her crying son as she puts the emergency oxygen equipment on him. Tears flood the mother's eyes. She puts the oxygen mask on herself and trembles. The mother clasps her hands and starts to pray. The child joins her.

The plane slams into the sea, shredding open the roof. Alexia and others fly out of the plane. Water crashes into the cabin, and the ocean waves slam into the mother and child. The plane explodes and sinks into the sea. Alexia flies through the air and slams into the water.

Above the crash site, a dark spirit hovers a mile above the wreckage. He glances, and some angels take people to heaven. Another evil spirit, named Murder, comes up to him.

"Status report," says the dark spirit named Death.

Murder gives Death a sheet of numbers and flies off. Death glances at the numbers. A bright light twinkles on the edge of his site. He turns his head. A bright angel swoops toward him.

Is that Michael? Death notices the angel's glowing white armor, platinum blond hair, and eyes full of red light. The angel approaches Death. "Oh, it's you," says Death. "What are you doing here, Satan? And in that form? Are you trying to relive the glory days?"

"Watch your tone, Death," says Satan sharply.

Death chuckles. "Or what? You'll kill me? Send me to the abyss?"

"Don't worry about how I look. I want to know how many people went to hell," says Satan. He grins at the thought.

"Out of a flight of three hundred, one hundred fifty went to hell."

Satan smiles and starts to chuckle. "How many survivors?"

"Ten. And the rest went to heaven," says Death.

Satan frowns. "Who survived, and why?"

"A few people from the crew, some passengers, and one person of note."

"Can you kill them?"

"Not at the moment."

"Why not?!"

"I have to set this stuff up correctly. Or I can't do it."

"I want them eaten by sharks. Can you do that?"

Death scans the area for sharks but sees two angels guarding the survivors, including the person of note. "Can't do it. Sorry."

Satan balls his fists and curses for two minutes. He exhales. "Who is this person of note that you mentioned before?" he asks. A smile flashes across his face.

Death turns his gaze toward the woman, who is now floating on a piece of airplane equipment. "Do you know a woman by the name of Alexia?"

Satan cradles his chin. "Ah. Alexia, Alexia," says Satan. He pauses. "I know about a thousand Alexias; you'll have to be more specific."

"The person on this flight was leaving the Central City area."

Satan's face frowns. *Hezekiah!* "I remember that she was Warlord's plaything. How did she escape the crash? Did you save her?"

"No," says Death. "I thought maybe you did."

Satan grits his teeth as Death reads the report.

"Ah. It says here that she was saved by an angel."

"What?" shouts Satan, throwing his hands into the air and letting them fall to his sides.

"It says here that she was running through the plane's cabin, looking for someone to pray for her."

"I don't believe it. God must be trying to reach her. I'll deal with Alexia later," says Satan as he balls his fists again.

"If you're not here for Alexia or anyone on this flight, then why are you here?"

"I'm here to talk to you."

"Talk to me? About what?"

Satan smiles. "Central City."

Death frowns. "Do you have permission for such an assignment?"

"No, but I'm about to get it. Where can I find you because you're not in one place very long?"

"I'll send someone to find you," says Death.

Satan turns to leave and looks back. "If you can, make sure the survivors die a horrible death."

"Probably not with those angels around."

Ignoring him, Satan flies straight up. He flies up so fast he beats the angels escorting spirits to the elevator leading to heaven. Satan gets on it, presses a button, and goes up. The elevator shoots out of the earth's atmosphere. It picks up speed and rockets out of the galaxy. Satan leans against the wall in the elevator; thinking of Hezekiah's bloody body on a pike puts a smile on his face. The elevator zips out of the galaxy and warps out of the universe.

The elevator door opens, and Satan steps out into heaven. He strolls towards heaven's gate and turns his head. The passengers of the plane crash stand in line at heaven's gate. A mother and her little boy stand in line and glance over.

"Mommy, who is that?" asks the little boy.

"That's Satan; don't look at him."

Satan ignores them and continues to walk toward the entrance.

Chapter 1

HIDDEN PLOT

IT'S EARLY MORNING IN THE TROPICAL DRY forest city of Central City. The sunlight streaks through the blue sky. The Spirit Warrior, Hezekiah, a golden-brown-skinned, athletically built warrior with black, curly hair, stands on the tan front porch of Dr. Frank Parker. He's there with Dr. Frank and his journalist daughter, Faith. A somewhat large crowd stands in front of them in the street, cheering for the former King Hezekiah, the city hero. Hezekiah's mouth dries. Moments before, the Holy Spirit had communicated sharply to his soul that the city is in danger. Seemingly in a trance, Hezekiah imagines what could come next.

"Hezekiah! Hezekiah? What are you daydreaming about? We have to get going," says Faith.

"I uh... where are we going again?" says Hezekiah, now lost in her light chocolate eyes.

"The governor's mansion, remember?" she says with a bright smile.

Meanwhile, Dr. Frank, a tan-skinned man with salt and pepper hair, motions to the crowd.

"Okay, folks. We appreciate your support, but Hezekiah needs his rest."

Out of understanding, the crowd disperses within minutes.

Frank gets the Jeep as Hezekiah and Faith stare at each other. Speechless, they hardly know what to say.

"Okay, you two love birds," Frank says as he drives up beside them. "The Jeep is ready. Let's go," he says with a smile.

Thinking about the ominous threat God gave Hezekiah and wondering what that threat could be, he keeps the warning to himself, for now, not wanting to worry his friends.

———————◆———————

Satan enters heaven's outer court. The place shines under the brilliance of God's light. He approaches a gold building and walks in. The high ivory walls panel the interior, and transparent gold tiles line the floor. He notices Jesus deep in the court putting something shiny in a chest. Jesus, preparing a special gift for Faith, hears Satan stroll into the inner court. Usually there to accuse, he approaches Jesus with a wicked smile on his face. An angel blows a trumpet and announces the devil's presence. Satan slows his approach. Jesus places the chest into an angel's hands. In a flash of light, He appears in front of Satan, and the devil trembles to his dark core.

"From where do you come, Satan?" says Jesus.

"I've come from roaming the earth."

"Oh. Is that all? And what questions do you have about Central City?" Jesus asks. The pressure of His presence drives Satan to his knees.

"I've... I've come to ask to kill Hezekiah."

"Really? You want to kill Hezekiah?" Jesus smiles. "You can kill him if he loses his will to fight."

Satan grits his teeth, and his muscles tighten. *Hezekiah losing his will to fight is like me losing my desire to kill him. He will never lose his will to fight.*

"If I can't kill him, then let me have Faith and all the other people in Central City," says Satan.

"And what do you want with Faith?"

"I want her dead."

"Okay," says Jesus.

Satan's jaw drops. "Really? Just like that? You're not going to say no?"

"I'm granting your request."

"And what about the other people in Central City? Can I do with them as I please?"

"Go."

Satan smiles and turns to leave His presence.

"However, Satan, you are not authorized to kill her with rape," says Jesus.

Satan frowns. "Then how can I kill her?"

"I'll let you figure that out. Only, she cannot be raped."

"Fine," says Satan with a huff.

"Oh, before you leave, Satan..." Satan turns around. "Do not take the elevator again. I noticed you forced My angels to escort My people to heaven the long way. You do that again, and I will make you feel an eternity of hell in the scope of a few seconds."

Satan gulps and slowly backs out of the court. The devil walks out and sees the mother and her son. The boy sticks his tongue out at him.

"Go away, Satan," says the little boy.

Satan ignores him and heads toward the portal leading to earth. Satan gazes at the blue portal that swirls like the entrance to the abyss. Satan jumps and thrusts through the portal. He quickly heads back to earth in search of his cohort, Death.

Hezekiah, Frank, and Faith get into the roofless Jeep and travel to the Governor's Mansion. Hezekiah notices how Faith's curly, dark, brown hair flows in the wind. The warm morning light cascades off her caramel skin.

I won't let anything happen to you. I don't know what I'd do if you died.

Faith gazes into Hezekiah's mahogany eyes and smiles. She reaches her hand across the tan seats. Hezekiah responds with his, and they hold hands. A tingling electric jolt sparks through their hands. "Why are you two so quiet all of a sudden?" says Frank from the driver's seat.

They both glance at Frank.

"You know, Hezekiah, just because you got the girl doesn't mean you stop talking to her. Also, Faith, I know you may be afraid of making a mistake as you transition from being great friends to being a romantic couple. Just remember, your relationship foundation is strong. It's centered on the Lord God."

"You're right, Dad," says Faith. "We've been through too much together in a short amount of time for us to be afraid of each other now."

"You're right. We love each other. And we both know it. We've already been through the fire in more ways than one. Our commitment to each other has been tested," says Hezekiah.

"I will say this, though," says Frank. "Continue to pursue and study each other. You will find out more about each other as you two become closer. Often, what causes relationships to fail is that spouses get used to each other and begin to take each other for granted."

"What do you mean?" asks Hezekiah.

"I'm talking about the cares of this world. For example, the stress of bills, work, and the pressures of life can take their toll on a romantic couple."

"I see what you are saying. So, we have to keep each other first," says Faith.

"No. You keep God first," says Frank. "When you keep God first, it will help you center your life. After God, then it's the two of you."

"Dad, where do you fit into all this positioning?"

"My beautiful daughter, if you two decide to get married, your spouse comes before me."

Hezekiah gazes into Frank's rear view mirror, and Frank meets his gaze. "Surprised, Hezekiah?" Well, for a marriage and family unit to work, spouses must focus on God and each other. If not, the relationship will fail. My daughter and I have a fantastic relationship, a relationship any father would dream of. However, I cannot monopolize your time away from Faith, Hezekiah. If I do, I'll turn into a hindrance."

"I see what you are saying. We won't have time for each other if we let outside pressure distract us," says Hezekiah.

"Also, if you are influenced by other men and women outside of the relationship, it can become a trap. Other men or women can try to distract you to break you two up. They will be interested romantically, offering something your spouse does not have, only to leave you with nothing in the end. Proverbs 5:3–6 says: 'For the lips of the adulterous woman drip honey, and her speech is smoother than oil; but in the end she is bitter as gall, sharp as a double-edged sword. Her feet go down to death; her steps lead straight to the grave. She gives no thought to the way of life; her paths wander aimlessly, but she does not know it.' This is a warning for women as well. There are a lot of Prince Charmings in the world who do exactly what Proverbs states."

"So, we must stay focused on each other, no matter what happens. Through good times and bad, we must stay faithful," says Hezekiah.

"Yeah," says Faith.

"I have a feeling that you two will not have a problem being committed to each other. However, with all this talk about relationships, I keep forgetting that you two aren't married yet."

Frank pulls up to the governor's mansion and parks the car. The large marble building stands out from the others. Polished concrete decorates the walk way and steps.

"This is a nice building," says Hezekiah.

Faith smiles, "Didn't you used to be a king? I'm sure you've seen better buildings than this."

They step out of the Jeep, onto the sidewalk, and walk up the stairs to the governor's mansion. They notice a doorman at the entrance.

"Do you have an appointment?" asks the doorman, named Paul. Paul's red uniform contrasts his pale skin.

"Yes, we are here to see Governor Roxbury," says Faith.

"And you are?"

Faith extends her hand for a handshake. "I'm Faith Parker, and this is my father, Frank Parker, and Hezekiah the Spirit Warrior."

Paul's eyes widen. "Oh, I recognize you now! How could I forget?" He shakes her hand.

Faith notices that his hands are clammy. She frowns, withdraws her hand, and wipes it on her pants. She takes a second look at the man and notices that he looks sick. "Are you okay?"

"Oh yeah! I'm fine. I just have a slight cold."

"Is a virus going around the office?" asks Faith.

"A few people are out of work sick, but it's nothing to worry about. Let me take you inside." Paul leads them inside.

The brown mahogany of the interior walls shine. Gold trim lines the walls of the hall. They walk on the tan tile floor making their way to the governor's office.

"I don't know if my mind is off today, but I'm a big fan of you, Hezekiah. Ever since your trial, I started to seek God in a real way."

"What makes you say that?" asks Hezekiah.

"I was a big fan of Warrington and the false gospel he was spreading. I was hooked onto the idea of sinning without consequence, the idea that God didn't care about how a person lived. However, when I saw the trial on television and witnessed Warrington turn into a demon on live television, I was horrified. I had started to really take stock of what he was saying about God. I asked God to lead me in the right direction, and He reminded me of what you said before in a prior debate with Warrington. You said God was a forgiving God, but He cared about how we lived. I started to read the Bible, and He told me in so many words that He would lead me into a relationship with Him and give me the Holy Spirit so sin would not have power over me."

"I'm glad that you gave your life to Christ during that trial. Sometimes you never know who is watching when you are going through a storm. That was a hard time in life for me. I'm glad that it ended up being a help for you too."

"Thank you. Well, here we are. Enjoy your meeting with the governor."

Chapter 2

THE CEREMONY

"AH, THE PARKERS! HOW ARE YOU DOING TODAY?" asks Governor Roxbury, a tanned, husky, older man with gray hair. He has on a crisp black suit and shoes, with a red tie. The window in his office allows the natural light to shine in.

"We're doing great. How are you, Governor?" asks Frank.

"I'm doing well. How are you doing, Hezekiah?"

"I'm doing well, sir," Hezekiah says, smiling.

"I invited you here because I wanted to thank you for saving the city. I also wanted to offer you a job."

"What kind of job, sir?"

"I wanted to offer you a job in city management. It's my understanding that you were a king at one point in time."

"Yes, I was. However, I don't have much interest in being in political power."

"It's not a political position. It's just a management position," says the governor.

Faith and Frank smile at Hezekiah.

"I'll have to pray about it first."

Both Frank and Faith frown.

"Understandable, Mr. Hezekiah. Let me know your decision. Now, about thanking you for your service... I want the three of you to follow me," says the governor.

The four leave the office and walk down the hallway. The governor's security detail ,secretary, and a few other staff members, follow them. A company of office staff follow the governor down the hallway toward the outer steps of the building.

"What's going on?" asks Faith.

"You'll see," says the governor. The governor's security detail open the outer doors of the mansion, and flash photography bombards them. Hezekiah notices broadcast cameras.

"What's going on?" asks Hezekiah.

"Hezekiah, I knew that you wouldn't let me do this if I told you about it in advance, so I decided to surprise you," says the governor.

The four walk down the stairs to a landing at the halfway point to be greeted by an attendant named Andrew. He holds three giant keys. A microphone and podium are set up. The governor walks behind the platform and adjusts the microphone.

"Dear fellow citizens of our great city. Thank you for coming on such short notice. In light of recent events, I wanted to officially recognize the people responsible for saving the city. Before me are three people who have shown true love, bravery, and courage in the face of danger. Frank Parker, with your skilled hands, you not only saved Hezekiah's life when he stayed in your home, but you also stood by him long enough for him to stand up for us. For that, we give you the key to the city."

Andrew hands Frank a key, and applause breaks out. Roxbury turns toward Faith.

"Faith, your determination in seeking the truth about the city of Phoenicia provided us with advance warning that we were dealing with a dangerous foe. Your journalism paved the way for Hezekiah to seek the full armor of God. For this, we also give you a key."

Andrew gives Faith a key, and the crowd applauds.

"And last, but certainly not least, Hezekiah, for your obedience to God and unfailing courage to stand up to Warrington, even amid the public upheaval and jeopardizing your safety, we applaud you. Because of your obedience to God, you saved the city from Warrington and his vast dark army. For the heroic acts that you have accomplished, we present you with a key to the city."

The crowd bursts into a fury of deafening applause. The governor shakes Hezekiah's hand and hugs him.

"Thanks so much." The governor slips something into Hezekiah's pocket and lets him go.

Andrew gives Hezekiah a key.

"Thank you so much, all three of you, for your selfless service." The governor, Hezekiah, Faith, and Frank walk back into the mansion.

Chapter 3

BREAKING THE ICE

AFTER THE CEREMONY, THE GOVERNOR GIVES THE trio an expensive change of clothes and limousine to go out on an all-expense-paid trip to an expensive restaurant. Hezekiah and Frank change into black suits, and Faith changes into a black dress. The governor arranges for a driver to drive the Parkers' Jeep back to their house. They get into the limousine and are taken to a bistro on the other side of town.

The bistro is lavishly decorated with chandeliers, curtains, and tables. The interior walls are tan in color. The tables and chairs are brown. The lights are subtly dim. The second floor has a terrace on each side of the restaurant. A frowning waiter meets them.

"Excuse me, do you have a reservation?" asks the waiter.

"Yes, we do; we are paid guests of the governor," says Hezekiah.

"Ah, it's Hezekiah and the Parkers. Honored guests. Come right this way." The waiter leads them to an inside table on the second floor. The view overlooks the mountains.

Hezekiah can't help notice how beautiful Faith looks. Her flowing curly hair and glowing skin energize him. Her elegant black dress accentuates her curvy athletic shape and fits the setting for the evening.

"You look lovely tonight, Faith," says Hezekiah.

"Thank you," she says.

They are quiet. Still getting used to dating, neither one is willing to make a relational mistake. The waiter walks up.

"Are you ready to order?"

"Yes," says Frank. "I'll have the chicken alfredo with a side of broccoli."

"And you, miss?" asks the waiter.

"I'll have the spinach and artichoke al forno."

"Good choice," says the waiter. "And you, sir?"

Hezekiah hesitates for a second. He lifts the menu to his face to cover his indecisiveness. *I can't believe this is happening to me.*

"I'll have the chicken alfredo as well." He does his best to sound confident. This lack of confidence catches him off guard. He is not used to feeling this way.

What is wrong with Hezekiah? Why is he acting like this? Faith thinks. *I hope this is not a continuing trend because timidity does not look good on him.*

Several minutes pass by, and no one says a word. Faith glances at her phone, and Hezekiah gazes toward the mountains.

Oh boy, this does not seem to be going well, Frank thinks. *I'd better break the Ice, or Hezekiah will end up in the good-friend zone.* "So, Hezekiah," says Frank. "What do you plan on doing now since your assignment is over?"

"I don't know, really. I guess I'm going to wait and see what God wants me to do next. I'm going to stay in town in case anything else happens."

"Do you think something else may happen?"

Not wanting to ruin dinner, Hezekiah hesitates to tell them, adding to the pressure. *Oh boy. I need to get my nervousness under control, or I'm going to fail at this relationship,* Hezekiah thinks.

The food arrives. *Whew, saved by the food.*

"Your dinner is served," says the waiter.

The trio begins to eat and enjoy themselves. Hezekiah composes himself. Hezekiah opens his mouth to speak, but Faith turns her head away. A tall man walks up to the table.

"Excuse me, miss?"

Faith looks up. Faith's eyes widen, and her jaw drops. Captivated by Faith from afar, a famous singer/actor named Sandstone comes over to talk to her.

"Can I sit down?" he asks. Sandstone has tan skin, brownish-blond hair, blue eyes, and a muscular physique. He has on a gold vest with no shirt, gold pants, and gold shoes. Hezekiah notices Faith's attraction to Sandstone.

"Sure!" says Faith.

Oh boy, here we go, thinks Frank.

As Sandstone sits down, Hezekiah gets up and walks off.

Faith's mind jolts from Sandstone to Hezekiah.

"Faith, I've been watching you on TV for a while, and I was wondering..."

Faith puts up her hand. "Excuse me, Sandstone." She gets up and follows Hezekiah. Hezekiah is across the room. "Hezekiah, wait," she says.

He keeps walking, pretending not to hear her until they reach the other side of the restaurant. They walk outside to the crisp cool air of the balcony with a view of the city. The city lights blaze brightly throughout the cityscape.

"Hezekiah, wait!"

He stops, rests his hands on the rail, and gazes over the city. Faith comes in close and holds his arm. She then rests her head on his shoulder. She notices his rock-hard shoulders. Knowing that she made a mistake, she thinks to defend herself but doesn't. Instead, she humbles herself.

"Hezekiah, I'm sorry," she says softly.

Hezekiah continues to gaze at the city below. She slowly turns him around and their eyes meet.

"I'm sorry, Hezekiah."

The Spirit Warrior gently holds her face. They stare into each other's eyes. He leans his face toward hers and kisses her. The one tentative touch of his lips against hers lights a spark that races through them both. One kiss becomes two, then a dozen. Through the pounding of their hearts in their ears, they both struggle within themselves, knowing they must stop.

Behind them, a glass falls and breaks, and they both jolt and stop kissing. The waiter apologizes to them and quickly moves on.

"Okay, we can't do that for too long. I love you, Faith, but we have to maintain control if we want to honor God," says Hezekiah.

Faith sighs. *I'm glad Hezekiah has discipline,* she thinks.

They compose themselves and walk back inside the restaurant, holding hands.

Sandstone has left Frank at the table.

"You left me here by myself to talk to Mister Sandstone. Is everything okay?" asks Frank.

"Sorry, Dad. Everything is fine."

Faith continues to talk, and Frank thinks: *Well played, Hezekiah, well played.*

Chapter 4

THE PROPOSAL

HEZEKIAH AND THE PARKERS ARE ON THEIR WAY
home. Frank and Faith talk among themselves about dinner. Hezekiah
silently prays to the Lord: *Lord Jesus, is this Your will for my life? Is it
Your will for me to marry Faith?*

Look inside your pocket.

Hezekiah checks his pocket and remembers that the governor gave
him something during the key to the city ceremony. There is a note
attached to the small item that reads:

Dear Hezekiah:

*I thank you from the bottom of my heart for what you and
your family have done for this city. Because of you, I have a
relationship with Jesus, and for that, I am eternally grateful.*

So please accept this token of my appreciation. I don't know the relationship between you and the Parkers, but I hope you enjoy it.

Thanks, beyond words,
Governor Roxbury

PS: The Limo and driver are available to you till the end of the week. Also, under the lining of this box is $500 and a check for $1000."

Hezekiah looks at the small item attached to the note and opens it. "Lord God, You speak so loudly without even speaking at all. Thank You, Jesus," he says.

"Hezekiah, did you say something?" says Faith.

"Oh, I was just praying," he says, grinning.

"What's that in your hand?" she asks.

Hezekiah shoots the item into his pocket. "It's just a gift from the governor."

"Well, can we see what it is?" asks Faith.

"In due time."

The limo approaches the house, and Hezekiah presses a button and requests the limo driver to make another stop. Fifteen minutes later, the limousine arrives outside of a well-lit nature trail. The trail goes uphill. At the top of the hill, the view overlooks their neighborhood. The limo driver steps out and opens the door for Faith. She steps out of the limo. Hezekiah moves toward the door, and Frank grabs his arm and whispers to him, "Hey, why are we here?" Hezekiah takes the item out of his pocket and shows Frank, holding his breath.

"I would be honored," says Frank.

Hezekiah smiles.

"Hezekiah, Dad, are you coming?" asks Faith.

"I'll be right there," says Hezekiah.

"I'm staying here. It's late. I want to take a nap in the limo," says Frank, as he winks at Hezekiah.

Hezekiah leaves the limo after Faith, and they walk up the brightly lit hill, holding hands.

Faith glances at him and notices his chiseled face and athletic shape. The moonlight causes his reddish-brown eyes to sparkle. Her stomach flutters. "Hezekiah, what is this about?"

"I'll let you know soon, my beautiful."

The two make it to the top of the hill and look at the great view of the brightly lit neighborhood.

"This is a beautiful view of our neighborhood. I'm glad we stopped here, but why did you bring me here?" she asks.

Hezekiah turns to her, gazes into her bright brown eyes, and gently grasps both of her hands. "Faith, I love you so very much. You have been there for me like no one has. You are very strong and magnificent. You are the most beautiful woman, inside and out, I have ever seen."

Her cheeks glow a rosy red. Her eyes twinkle in the star-lit night.

"Even more so, your love for God is awesome. You trust God amid danger. That quality you have makes you far more attractive. You have a fearlessness I have not seen in anyone else." Hezekiah gets down on one knee, and Faith gasps and her eyes widen. "Faith, will you marry me?"

Images of Hezekiah's dedication and loving friendship flash through her mind. The Bible studies, walking through the forest, and eating ice cream together causes her to smile. The time he put his life on the line to save her from Warlord, and the time he remained locked up for her make her heart skip a beat. Traveling into the abandoned garrison with him to search for the shield of faith causes tingles to travel through her chest. The moment she forgave him for killing her mother, or so she thought, makes her mouth go dry. As she recalls pleasant and tough moments, with an overflow of her heart, her mouth speaks, "Yes, Hezekiah. Yes!" as she puts her hand over her mouth. Her knees buckle.

Hezekiah pops up and hugs her. Faith hugs him back, and their lips touch and lock onto each other. Fluttering flows through their faces. They pull back. They gaze into each other's eyes, and Frank walks up.

"Congratulations, you two! I can't think of a better couple," says Frank.

They both nod and smile. Their faces gleam in the moonlight.

"I'm so glad you two are getting married because I was starting to worry for a second."

"What do you mean?" asks Faith.

"Don't worry about it," he says as he thinks of talking to Hezekiah later. The trio walks down the hill in high spirits. They get into the limo and head for home.

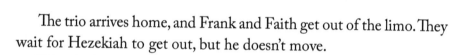

The trio arrives home, and Frank and Faith get out of the limo. They wait for Hezekiah to get out, but he doesn't move.

"Hezekiah, what's wrong?" asks Frank. "The limo has to go back by a certain time, I'm sure."

Hezekiah is silent for a moment, not knowing how to phrase what he must say next.

"What is it?" asks Faith.

Hezekiah exhales. "I'm sorry, but I can't stay here any further."

"What?" says Faith and Frank.

"It has nothing to do with you, or maybe it does. Faith, the way I feel about you now, we can't stay in the same house without us doing something we shouldn't."

"Oh, okay. I understand fully," says Frank.

"What do you mean? Oh," says Faith, blushing.

"Where are you going to stay then?" asks Frank.

"Well, the governor gave me a sum of money at the press ceremony, so I'm going to stay at a residential inn so I can get on my feet."

"Okay, that's understandable," says Frank.

"I'll call you when I get to my new place," says Hezekiah.

"Okay," says Faith softly.

Hezekiah closes the door of the limo, and the driver drives off into the night.

Chapter 5

LONGING

THE NEXT DAY, FAITH AND FRANK AWAKEN. FAITH leaves her room, wishing that Hezekiah was lying next to her. She gets up, and out of habit, goes to Hezekiah's old room and opens the door. Of course, he is not there. Looking down at the floor, she wishes her love was there with her.

"Good morning, Faith. What's wrong?" asks Frank.

"Oh, nothing. I just wish Hezekiah were here too."

"Don't worry about it. It was for a good reason."

"What makes you say that?"

"Well, for starters, you two are not married, and you're a couple who is madly in love with each other. It would only be a matter of time before you two..."

"Before we what, Dad?" Faith says, forming a smile.

"Must I really say it, sweetie? Even though I see Hezekiah as family, I still don't want to imagine you two together in that way."

"What? Making love?" says Faith, now giggling.

"Faith!"

"What, Dad? We're both adults here. I figure we could talk about this."

"Okay, since you want to play it that way. Let me tell you what your mom and I did on our honeymoon. We had only just arrived to the suite room when she—"

"Okay! Okay! I get the point," says Faith.

"That's what I thought. Anyway, what I'm trying to say is that sometimes, no matter how spiritual you are, temptation can get the best of you. As Christians, we have a reputation to worry about."

"Why should we have to worry about what people think? We are in love with each other, and we're getting married anyway."

"That's not the point."

"Well, what is the point?" asks Faith.

"The point is it will bring dishonor to God's name. Hezekiah is the Spirit Warrior, and you are a known Christian reporter. People would either frown at you two, or they would become emboldened to do what they want. We just had a major battle against Warlord and his lies. Do we really want to go through that again?"

"Okay, I get your point. But still, that doesn't stop the way I feel about him," says Faith, plopping on the couch.

"Well, that's why you get married," says Frank.

"That reminds me. Why didn't we set a date?"

"Because he needs to find a job."

The phone rings. Faith rushes to the house phone and picks it up. "Hello?"

"Is this Faith Parker?"

"Yes, it is."

"Your vehicle warranty—"

Click.

"Who was that?" asks Frank.

"A telemarketer," she says. The phone rings again. She picks it up slowly. "Hello?" she says plainly.

"Hey, beautiful. How are you doing?" asks Hezekiah.

Faith's face brightens. "I'm doing great. Where are you?"

"I'm out and about, looking for employment. I'm on my way to the governor's mansion to look for a job."

"That's great! What are you looking to do?"

"Anything I can to take care of you."

Faith blushes. "So, when are you coming over?"

"It will be this afternoon after I'm done job hunting."

"Okay. We need to talk when you come."

"Okay. Well, I've got to go. I'm on my way into the mansion now. So, I'll talk to you soon. I love you," says Hezekiah.

"I love you too," she says. Faith hangs up the phone.

"So where is he?" asks Frank.

"Going to the Governor's Mansion to get a job for me."

"I wonder what job God will give him," says Frank.

"What makes you say that?"

"Well, he has to have something that will allow him to have time with God, you, and protecting the city."

"That's a good point. I hope he finds the right job."

Chapter 6

DEAD ENDS

HEZEKIAH WALKS INTO THE GOVERNOR'S MANSION. Through prayer the night before, he discovered a way to transform his armor into any type of clothing he could think of. He also found out a cool trick: if he wears the armor cloaked as regular clothing, not only will the armor not disappear after a battle, but the recovery time for using the full armor again is seconds instead of minutes. If he has to summon it from afar, the armor disappears after the battle and comes back one piece at a time. The only thing is if he wears the armor regularly, his clothing will only be white or gold, a side effect he does not mind, as long as he can always keep on the armor.

Hezekiah walks into the Governor's Mansion to the front desk to talk to Andrew.

"Hezekiah, I was not expecting you today. How are you doing?" his new friend says above a whisper.

"I'm doing great. Is there any way I can speak to the governor?" says Hezekiah.

"Well, he is in a meeting right now. What is it about?"

"It's about the job he proposed to me yesterday," he says, straightening his collar.

"Oh, the management position."

"Is that still available?"

"No. He filled that position yesterday."

"What?"

"Yes. He really needed someone for that position. After you turned it down, someone showed up yesterday, interviewed for it, and got the job. I'm so sorry. If I had known you were interested, I would have told the governor."

"That's okay. Are there any more positions available?"

"Unfortunately, no. I'm sorry."

Hezekiah leaves the mansion and goes around the city searching for a job. Hours pass by. From fast food to industrial, no work is too big or small for him. However, what Hezekiah doesn't know is that God is closing every single door he tries to walk through.

Finally, out of desperation, Hezekiah prays out loud: "Lord God, why can't I find a job?"

Because you already have one.

"What?" asks Hezekiah. God doesn't say another word. It's now late afternoon. To keep his promise, Hezekiah heads to Faith's house.

Chapter 7

HELP MATE

HEZEKIAH ARRIVES AT THE PARKERS' HOUSE AND rings the doorbell. Disappointed at how the day went, he tries to cover it up by putting on a fake smile. Faith opens the door.

"Hey, Hezekiah! How was your day?"

"It was good."

She sees through Hezekiah's façade. "What's wrong? Did you find anything?"

"No, I didn't."

"That's okay. Come let's go to the backyard and talk."

Hezekiah and Faith walk through the house into the backyard. They both sit down on a boulder. Faith has a basket of food set up so he can eat. They eat and enjoy themselves as the sun sets in the sky.

"That's beautiful, isn't it?" says Faith, softly.

The sunlight reflects off of her chocolate eyes. "It's not as beautiful as you."

She blushes and grazes her hand across his fingers that sends warmth across his hand.

Hezekiah puts his head down. "Faith. I didn't know it would be so difficult to find a job. I have years of executive management experience, and I can't even get a job at a fast-food restaurant."

"Did you ask God for help?"

"Yes."

"Well, what did He say?"

"He said that I already had one."

Faith thinks for a moment. "I'll be right back. Wait here."

Hezekiah raises an eyebrow and smiles as Faith disappears into the house. Faith comes back outside with a Bible in her hand.

"Okay, let's see," she says as she flips through the Bible. "Okay, here we go. In Proverbs 18:16, it says: 'A gift opens the way and ushers the giver into the presence of the great.'"

"So, what are you saying?" asks Hezekiah.

"What I'm saying is that you are in a situation where God no longer wants you to work a job for you to survive. He wants you to work your gift."

"Which is?"

"Duh, you are the Spirit Warrior!"

He thinks for a second. "I see what you are saying, but I can't make money for being a superhero."

"You're thinking about this all wrong. You have a great understanding of the scriptures and an ability to use them in a crisis. Have you ever thought about applying to the church for a ministry position?"

Hezekiah smiles.

"Even if they don't hire you, you could start your own ministry based on your knowledge of the scriptures alone."

"You are a genius!" Hezekiah gets up and kisses her. Warmth escapes his lips and flows through hers. The sensation swarms through her lips and across her face. She struggles to take a breath. Hezekiah pulls back. "You are a true friend."

Faith exhales and softly puts her hand on his chest. "Good. We can go to the church tomorrow and talk to Pastor Brian and Lisa. Now get out of here before we do something we shouldn't," says Faith.

Hezekiah goes to his place, and Faith goes to bed alone.

Chapter 8

THE AUDITION

IT'S A FROSTY MORNING. HEZEKIAH AND FAITH both meet at Central City Church. The yellow stucco siding of the church gives the area a warm glow. Hezekiah, not dressed in any of the armor but the shoes, wears a brown overcoat, white-collar shirt, and khaki pants. Faith wears a red dress and a thin white jacket. They kiss and exchange greetings. They walk toward the entrance of the church. As they walk, Hezekiah recalls the evil influence that Warlord had over this church. Warlord, under the guise of Lloyd Warrington, had been Pastor Brian's spiritual advisor for years before Hezekiah exposed him for the devil he was. Consequently, it revealed that Pastor Brian, at the time, wasn't a Christian. But a good speaker in a leadership position, guided by a demon.

"It's hard to believe this church was spiritually dead not too long ago," says Hezekiah, frowning.

"I know. If it weren't for you and your grand stand against Warlord, this congregation, along with a lot of people in the city would be in hell."

"How did Pastor Brian get reinstalled as pastor over the church? I thought he was removed."

"After Warlord was exposed, the church thought it would be a good idea for a familiar face to lead the congregation."

"I like Pastor Brian, but he's a new Christian himself. Can he handle the spiritual responsibility of being a pastor?"

"Let's face it, everyone in this city who is a follower of Christ, with the exception of my dad and us, are either new to the faith, don't know enough about the Bible, or are lukewarm. There is no one else. Perhaps you're here to help him grow."

They arrive at the entrance and ring the buzzer at the door, which has a camera. "Can I help you?" asks a lady through the speaker on the buzzer.

"Hey, we are here to meet with Pastor Brian and Mrs. Lisa," says Faith.

"Do you have an appointment?"

"No."

"I can't get you in without an appointment."

Hezekiah buzzes the button. "Hello, miss?"

"Is that Hezekiah the Spirit Warrior?" she says, voice squeaking.

"Yes, ma'am," says Hezekiah.

"Why didn't you say so? Come on in," says the woman.

Faith glances at Hezekiah, raises an eye brow, but smiles.

The attendant escorts Faith and Hezekiah to the sanctuary. The sanctuary is a big auditorium complete with red movie theater-style seats. The church band is currently on stage getting ready for rehearsal. The pastor is on stage, discussing something with his wife.

"Hezekiah!" Pastor Brian calls when he sees the two visitors. "How are you doing today?"

"I'm doing great, Pastor Brian, how are you and your wife doing?"

"We're doing well, thank you for asking."

"I don't mean to pry, but how did you two..."

"Get back together? After my kiss with Alexia? It's simple. She forgave me."

"Okay. How is your relationship with God?"

"It's going great. I'm still learning what it means to follow Christ, but by no means am I pretending to be a pastor like I did before. Thank you, again, for leading me to a real relationship with God."

"Thank God."

"So, what brings you here today?" asks Pastor Brian.

"I wanted to know if you had any job openings here," says Hezekiah.

"Really? Well, God must have led you here because we were just talking about a vacancy we need to fill."

"Okay, what does it involve?"

"You may have to do clerical work on occasion. And the youth pastor may need help at times too. However, there is a primary skill you need to have."

"Which is?"

"Are you good at singing? We are looking to fill the position 'Pastor of Worship.' We know that you are a Christian, you have years of leadership experience, you're great with people, and you're well versed in the Bible. The only thing we need to know is, can you sing?"

"Yes, actually," says Hezekiah. Faith's eyes widen. *What?*

"I consider myself a tenor based on the songs I used to sing along with the radio. But, It's been a while, though. In fact, I don't think I've actually sung a song in front of anyone before."

"Well, if you can't, I'm sure that there are other positions in the church I could give you."

"No wait, let me try." Hezekiah walks on stage and timidly grabs a microphone. His hands shake slightly. Some of the band members on stage look at Hezekiah and sneer.

Pastor Brian, Lisa, and Faith look on as they wait for Hezekiah to do something.

"Is that the Spirit Warrior?" asks one of the musicians coming out of the restroom. He yells out into the hall: "The Spirit Warrior is about to sing on stage! Come quick!" People near the auditorium stop what they're doing and enter inside. The church staff gathers as they see Hezekiah on stage with a microphone in his hand. Hezekiah's nerves are now set on edge. The onlookers watch, breath in their throat.

Does he really know how to sing, thinks Lisa.

The stage crew shines a light on Hezekiah, and the room goes dark. *Father God, what should I sing?*

He looks down among the seats at Pastor Brian, Lisa, and Faith, but Faith is gone. Hezekiah frowns and exhales. A warm wind gushes inside of his soul, and he exhales.

"Amazing grace, how sweet the sound that saved a wretch like me." Hezekiah starts to crescendo, and he hears a beautiful alto voice off to his right.

He looks over, and Faith is singing. They continue to sing together. The church staff applauds and cheers. Their singing takes on resonance. Both voices powerfully echo throughout the auditorium, and the atmosphere changes to one of worship. The Spirit of God enters the room, and people raise their hands and sing along. Hezekiah and Faith stare into each other's eyes while harmonizing. They slowly bring the song to a close and the church staff hoots and applauds.

Pastor Brian and Lisa walk on stage. "I didn't know you two could sing that well!" says the pastor. "I think this goes without saying, but the job is yours."

Faith and Hezekiah continue to stare into each other's eyes as if the pastor didn't say a word.

Chapter 9

ONE MORE STEP

HEZEKIAH AND FAITH LEAVE THE CHURCH AND walk toward her Jeep.

"Hezekiah, I didn't know you could sing like that! When did you learn how to sing?"

"I don't know. I just used to sing when I would hear a song on the radio. When did you learn how to sing?"

"I used to sing in the choir when I was a little girl. I tried to continue as a teenager, but my parents started medical missions, and I lost interest in the choir."

"You should definitely continue. I love the way you vocalize."

"Really?"

"Yeah, you sing like a beautiful bird and with the power of a lioness," says Hezekiah. Faith blushes.

"You have a powerful singing voice as well. I see this was a God thing because that position for worship leader is perfect for you."

"Thank you. It seems to be perfect for you too. We should sing together more often."

"We should, and we will," says Faith, staring into Hezekiah's eyes.

Smiling, Hezekiah asks, "Faith, what are you thinking about?"

"You know, you have a career now."

"Yes. So..."

"So, I was thinking, what are we waiting for?"

"That's right! We could get married now!" Hezekiah says. "No, wait, I need to get a place to live."

"You could just move back in with my dad and me," says Faith. They make it to the Jeep. Faith sits on the hood of the Jeep, and Hezekiah stands near her.

"As much as I wouldn't mind that, I can't do it. I really want to get a place of my own. I know it may be a male ego-type deal, but I think it's important that I get my own house first."

Faith stands and lays her hand over his heart. "You know, the more I get to know you, the more you impress me without even trying."

Hezekiah frowns slightly. "What do you mean?"

"You are just so mature and responsible. You don't play the games that men play. You are different, in a good way."

"Thank you."

"Did your parents raise you this way?"

"Yes, they did," he says, turning his head away, putting his hand over his eyes.

Faith draws closer and puts her arms around his waist. "I didn't mean to—"

"No, it's okay. I don't want to be an emotional wreck around you whenever my parents are mentioned."

"Hezekiah, have you forgiven yourself for what happened?"

"I thought I did, but it's just so hard," Hezekiah says.

Faith softly grabs his chin and brings him back to face her. They softly look into each other's eyes for a few seconds.

She says gently, "Hezekiah, you were different back then. You were a man for the devil when your parents died. But now, you are a child of God. God loves you, and He has forgiven you. Your parents are with God, and I'm sure, beyond a shadow of a doubt, that they are proud of you."

Hezekiah smiles. "And that right there is one of the many reasons why I love you."

"What do you mean?" asks Faith.

"You're so caring and compassionate. It's unreal," says Hezekiah with a chuckle.

"Stop it. Other people are compassionate."

"Not like you, Faith. At least, not to me." Hezekiah takes advantage of their close proximity and gives her a quick peck on the lips. She laughs and kisses him right back a little longer. A surge of pulsating warmth envelops their lips and faces. He pulls back. "We've got to marry soon," he says. "It's getting harder and harder to resist you."

"I feel the same way. Find a place soon." Hezekiah turns and walks toward the limo. "Wait, where are you staying now?" asks Faith.

"I'm staying at an extended stay hotel. I have enough until my first paycheck."

"Maybe you won't have to wait that long," she says. A smile crosses her face.

"What do you mean?"

"My dad has some property near the forest."

"What? How come you didn't say anything about it before?" he says, scratching his head.

"Well, between the city almost being destroyed and demons running wild everywhere, I think the thought slipped my mind."

"Good point," he says. "So how much do you think he will sell it for?"

"I don't know, let's ask him and see."

Chapter 10

FINAL STEP

FRANK IS OUT ON THE BACK PORCH. HEZEKIAH and Faith pull up in the jeep. The limo driver parks the limo behind the Jeep. They both get out and walk toward the house.

"Hey! How is the happy couple?" asks Frank, smiling. Hezekiah approaches him and shakes his hand firmly. "You look all dressed up. Did you go on an interview today?"

"Yes, I did, and I got the job," says Hezekiah smiling.

"Congratulations! So, what will you be doing for a living?"

"I am a worship leader."

Frank cocks his head back and raises an eye brow. "You're a worship leader?"

"Yeah."

"Don't worship leaders sing?" he asks, squinting.

"Yes, sir, they do."

"Hezekiah, you know how to sing?"

"Yes, Dad, and he sings really well."

Frank is speechless. "I didn't peg you as the type to sing. Can you sing me a tune?"

"Dad, Hezekiah has an important question to ask you."

"Well, what is it?" he asks.

"I wanted to know how much you would sell your vacation house for," asks Hezekiah.

"My what?" Frank scratches his head. "Oh. It's been a while since I've been there. I hope it's in good condition."

"If it is, how much would you sell it for?" asks Hezekiah.

"I will give you the house for free," says Frank.

Hezekiah's face brightens and then he frowns. "No, as good as that sounds, I want to do this the right way and buy the house from you."

Frank glances at Faith and looks Hezekiah in the eyes. "I know what you are trying to do. I know that you want to be the man and provider for Faith, but you must understand something. God is the true provider. He is the one who 'opens doors that no man can shut and shuts doors that no man can open.' How do you think you got the money to stay at an extended stay in the first place? It wasn't from your own job; that was God's handiwork. How do you think you got the ring to propose with? Or how do you think you landed the dream job at the church? God has given you these things for a reason. He gave you the extended stay so you wouldn't fall into sin with my daughter. He gave you money to survive until you got the job at the church. You're at the church to be a beacon of light to point to Jesus, and now God is giving you a house you and your wife can live in. Don't try to refuse it because you know what I am saying is true."

Hezekiah puts his head down and smiles. His eyes soften and moisten. "Thank you."

"You're welcome, but most importantly, thank God, because I've meant to sell that house. The thought of selling it kept slipping my mind because something more important took precedence. Now I know why I didn't sell it. It's to be a house for you and my daughter," says Frank, smiling.

"Thanks, Frank," says Hezekiah. He shakes Franks hand firmly.

"Well, the day is still young. Let's go see the house," says Frank, smiling.

Chapter 11

HAUNTED HOUSE

THE TRIO, IN THEIR RESPECTIVE VEHICLES, DRIVE into the woods on the outskirts of the city and arrive at a two-story modern farmhouse, yellow with a red terracotta roof.

"This is a nice size house!" says Hezekiah.

"You know, If I didn't know any better, I wouldn't think you were a king in your past life," says Frank.

"How can you afford this?" asks Hezekiah.

Frank looks at him sideways. "Don't insult me. You do remember that I'm a medical doctor, right?"

"Oh, right."

"Anyway, I bought this house when I was still working at the hospital. It's fully furnished. I used to have a maid service clean this place when I vacationed here."

"Why did you stop coming to the house?"

"I stopped coming here because my wife and I used to vacation here."

"Oh," says Hezekiah.

"This place was a getaway for my wife and me. I used to bring Faith here after she was born. But after my wife died, I just couldn't come here anymore. She loved this house. Being here reminds me of her. Staying in this house by myself would just be too painful."

"I see."

"Which is why I'm glad to be giving this house over to you. She would be happy to know that this house now belongs to her daughter," says Frank, eyeing the farmhouse.

The trio wanders toward the house. Hezekiah sees something from the corner of his eye. The hairs on the back of his neck stand up. He turns his head sharply but sees nothing. Faith steps toward Hezekiah.

"Hezekiah, what's wrong?" asks Faith, her pulse picking up.

He exhales. "It's nothing. I just thought I saw something. That's all," says Hezekiah, frowning.

"Don't scare us like that. We've all been through too much for you to do stuff like that," says Faith sharply.

"It's okay," says Frank. He chuckles and puts a hand on Faith's shoulder. "Let's just calm down, go inside, and see what's what."

The three go inside and find dust everywhere. Faith starts to sneeze and cough.

"It's so dusty in here. This place needs to be cleaned out," she says. She gags, coughing up mucus. Her head starts pounding. Hezekiah puts his hands on her shoulders. "Jesus," he says. Faith's body energizes from the inside out and her headache disappears. Frank moves in closer.

"My goodness, Faith, you're scaring me," says Frank. "I'll tell you what. Just stay on the porch where I can see you and I'll rummage through the house." He takes a handkerchief out of his pocket and wipes her face. She grabs it from him and smiles. She spits mucus into the cloth and throws it into a nearby trash can. Hezekiah rubs her back and turns his gaze toward Frank.

"I wanted to know if we could go around to the backyard and see what it looks like," says Hezekiah.

"Okay. Just go around back and I'll look through the house."

"Actually, Dad, I want to look through the house with you," says Faith.

"Are you sure you'll be okay?"

"Yeah, Dad, I'll be fine. Just let me put a scarf around my face." Faith reaches into her purse and holds a scarf to her face.

"Okay, dear. Hezekiah, I guess you can go check out the backyard and we'll be in here looking around," says Frank.

Hezekiah walks away as he hears Faith say, "I thought that a cleaning company was supposed to be here to clean."

"I stopped paying them. We'll just have to call them to come back," says Frank.

Hezekiah walks out into the open backyard and breathes the fresh air. He looks for a good place for Spirit sword training. The grass is a little overgrown but not too much, and the backyard leads to a wooded area.

He walks through the backyard and hears a strange, loud whisper through the trees. The hairs on his arms stand up. He slows. He walks a little farther into the backyard and notices a working fountain under a stone gazebo. *Maybe that was just the sound of the rushing water.*

Whispers flood his ears above the sound of the fountain. The sound seems to emanate from the tree line. He walks a little farther and goes into the forest. A clearing opens his way into the tree line.

Okay, there's nothing here.

The Spirit Warrior unsheathes the sword of the Spirit from within his soul just in case. Hezekiah hears the loud whisper, farther into the forest. He takes a step, and a twig breaks behind him. Hezekiah turns his head. A pale ghost is rushing toward the house!

"No!"

Hezekiah rockets out of the forest. The ghostly figure takes off from the ground and jumps into the air toward the house. The ghoul flies toward the upstairs window and has Faith in its sights. Hezekiah soars past it, spins, and strikes. Wind blasts from his sword. The ghost is hit by the force and shoots back into the forest. Hezekiah bounces off the house and flies through the air toward the forest.

Faith and Frank notice the sound and look out the window but see nothing. They continue to investigate the house.

Hezekiah soars through the tree line after the ghost. He flips through the air and lands and slides across the ground to a stop. Hezekiah hears more loud whispers. The murmuring voices turn into screams. A fire blast strikes Hezekiah's back. Hezekiah flies through the forest. He pushes against the force of the blast and spins out of it. He grabs his burning brown coat and tosses it away. His feet touch the ground and slides to a stop, facing the ghost. The ghost charges at him. Hezekiah flinches. The ghost cocks his sword and strikes. A fire blast echoes from its sword. Hezekiah leaps backward. Hezekiah slices the blast to the ground. Fire jumps on his shirt. His shirt catches fire and he rips it away. He looks back, slams into a boulder, and collapses to the ground.

Hezekiah shakes his head and looks up at the ghost and smirks. The evil spirit forms fiery red armor around himself, and his sword turns red. The heat of its armor touches Hezekiah's skin, and he starts to sweat. Hezekiah zips toward his opponent. The evil spirit counters, and they clash swords. Hezekiah slashes at him from various angles, and the demon blocks. The tempo of their clashes skyrockets. They fight through the forest, clashing blades. The Spirit Warrior uppercuts, but the creature dodges. The ghost electrifies his sword and strikes. A fire blast hits the swordsman. It knocks Hezekiah through a tree. Pain spikes through Hezekiah's back. The shattered timber is set ablaze. The ghost volleys more explosions of heat. Hezekiah darts out the way of each burst. Heat and smoke travel into Hezekiah's lungs. Hezekiah's insides start to burn. He exhales hard. He gets low to the ground and takes a full breath. He holds his breath as he leaps off the ground while avoiding a fire blast. Part of the forest flashes into an inferno.

Frank and Faith look out of the window and see the forest on fire. They hear loud clashing in the forest.

Hezekiah and the ghost continue to fight through the blazing forest. Hezekiah's air starts to run out. His insides burn from lack of air. With a wall of flames around them, the ghost thrusts toward Hezekiah. Hezekiah blocks. The ghost hits Hezekiah. The impact thrusts Hezekiah into the air. Hezekiah back smacks into a boulder. Air escapes Hezekiah's mouth. The Spirit Warrior falls to his knees, coughing. The ghost laughs. He walks toward Hezekiah. The ghost's sword starts to flare with power. He strolls toward the Spirit Warrior.

Hezekiah coughs. His lungs start to burn from lack of oxygen. He looks at the ghost slowly approaching and sees double. Coughing and blinking, Hezekiah's heart thuds in his chest.

"God, help."

The Holy Spirit ignites inside of Hezekiah's soul. The swordsman's blade explodes into a blue fire-saber. Hezekiah gulps in air and holds his breath. The Spirit Warrior zips off the ground and strikes; a blast of blue fire explodes from his sword. The ghost is hit. It rockets across the forest. Lungs burning, Hezekiah pursue. The swordsman rockets and catches up to the ghost. Hezekiah slices through the demon's armor. Part of the armor blows to pieces. Hezekiah slices the ghost from all directions. Lungs burning, Hezekiah's face turns red. He strikes the ghost. A blue explosion booms from his sword. The ghost slides backward but is still on his feet. The ghost's armor starts to disintegrate. From above, Hezekiah slices down through the ghost's armor, and it screams. The ghost lifts its sword, and Hezekiah slices straight through it. The ghost turns to run, and Hezekiah slices through the demon multiple times and slashes with a fire blast. The ghost sails across the ground a short distance. Hezekiah zips and slashes straight through the ghost's abdomen and slides to a stop a short distance away.

Amidst fire, the ghost's armor falls off, and he falls to his knees and screams. Hezekiah turns around and glances at the ghostly figure. The ghost forces himself to stand. Spirit flesh popping, the ghost whimpers. He grits his teeth, coughs, and smiles. He turns around to face Hezekiah. "Faith is a dead woman walking," he says. He starts to laugh and gags. Hezekiah strikes with a blast of light; the blast hits the ghost and disintegrates him.

Chapter 12

AFTERMATH

FRANK AND FAITH RUN TOWARD THE FOREST. The prickly heat hits them, and they stop.

"Faith, call the fire department now!" The crackling flame roars through the forest.

Faith checks herself for her cell phone.

"Faith!" Frank points into the sky.

Hezekiah ascends into the air. He slashes the air. Lightning explodes from his sword. Thunder booms. A torrent of rain falls toward the forest. Hezekiah descends out of view. The rain slams down into the flames. The fire crackles, hiss, and goes out. Frank and Faith run into the charry woods. Hezekiah, a short distance away, walks, using hot trees for support.

"Hezekiah! Hezekiah! Are you okay?" shouts Faith. She puts her arms around him.

Hezekiah coughs.

"Yes, I'm fine," says Hezekiah, gazing into her eyes, smiling.

"What happened out here?" asks Frank.

"I was fighting a ghost."

"What?" says Faith.

"Yeah. I came out to the backyard to find a good spot for practicing with the sword. However, I kept hearing a loud whisper. Anyway, it lured me into the forest. I just happened to look back, and I saw that spirit rushing toward the house. I cut it off at the pass by striking it into the forest. I then bounced off the house to springboard into the forest."

"So that was the loud boom we heard against the house."

"Yes. Anyway, we fought, and I slew it. However..." Hezekiah hesitates.

"What is it?" asks Frank, frowning.

"Hezekiah, we've been through too much for you to keep secrets from us now. Trust me, we can handle it," says Faith.

He glances at both of them and settles on Frank. "The evil spirit said, 'Faith is a dead woman walking.'"

Both Frank and Faith gasp.

"Great. Another demonic spirit after my daughter," says Frank, throwing his hands in the air.

"Dad. Don't worry," says Faith. "Don't you worry either, Hezekiah. We have been through this before, and I'm quite sure you will protect me. Remember Warlord? Well, he didn't kill me."

"Yeah, that's true," says Hezekiah.

"I have complete confidence that you'll protect me. Besides, if it's really my time to die, I'll be okay," she adds with a smile.

Frank and Hezekiah's eyes widen. "Faith, don't say that," they say.

"What? I would be okay. I would go straight to heaven."

"Yes, but we're not ready to lose you," says Hezekiah. His hand cups hers. "I'm not ready to lose you."

"I don't want to lose you either," she says. "But it's something I have to think about every day when you go out into battle."

"Why are we talking about death so much? We need to find out what is going on and figure out a way to stop whatever it is," says Frank.

"You're right. We're not going to let some demon dictate whether or not someone dies," says Faith.

Chapter 13

SLEEPLESS NIGHT

HEZEKIAH IS AT THE HOTEL. THE GHOST'S WORDS about Faith, hours before, haunts him. He rubs the back of his neck thinking about worst-case scenarios. He lies down. Tossing and turning, not able to get comfortable, Hezekiah claps his hands.

"Lord, please protect Faith. I may not be there every second of the day, but You are. Please protect her. In Jesus's name, amen."

Hezekiah exhales, blinks his eyes, and closes them. His breathing relaxes. Faith is hit by a car! He snaps back awake and gets on the phone to call her.

———————⋄———————

Asleep, Faith hears her cell phone buzzing. The phone pitter patters across the bed toward the edge. She picks it up. Groggy, she rubs her eyes and licks her lips to speak.

"Hello?" she says.

"Hey, is everything okay over there?" asks Hezekiah.

"Yeah, everything is fine. Are you still worried about me?" she asks softly.

"Of course, I am."

"I know, but I can't ask you to come over here."

"Why not?" asks Hezekiah.

"Because it's the middle of the night, and I've kind of been waiting for our wedding night for a while, if you know what I mean."

"Oh... Well, I can post up on the roof."

"That won't work because then I won't sleep. I'll end up coming up there and give you some food to eat. Then we'll probably strike up a conversation. We'll both notice how beautiful the moonlit night is and then we'll hold each other."

"Okay. Keep going."

"Then we'll probably kiss. Then we'll stop to honor God. Then I'll offer you something to eat, and you'll follow me inside."

"And then what?"

"Hezekiah, I've been waiting for a wedding night long before I met you. I've been saving this moment for my whole short life."

"Wait, are you a..."

"Yes. I'm a virgin."

"Oh, okay. So am I."

"Wait, what? But I thought you used to be an evil king."

"I was, but I never had enough time to do anything with another woman because I was always involved in some sort of conflict. After a while, women were too afraid to even come close to me, so I just focused on ruling the kingdom."

"What about in high school?" she asks.

"I was the school outcast. No one was interested in me."

"Okay, what about in college?"

"I didn't have time for college. That's when I started to rule the kingdom.

"Okay. I get it. That means our first will be extra special," says Faith. "Just take things slow and be gentle because I don't want our first night together to be a horror story."

"There won't be a first time for us if you die before we get married. Not that our making love is the only reason why I want you alive. I don't want to lose you, period. You are the only person I've ever fallen in love with."

Faith's heart skips a beat. "Hezekiah, there is no way you could be around me every second of the day. You are just going to have to trust God on this one, okay?"

Hezekiah is silent for a moment.

"I know you don't want to see me go away, but if it's my time to go, it's just my time," says Faith.

"I know, but I still don't want to lose you."

"Let's stop talking about losing each other. We are going to get married soon. Let's focus on spending the rest of our lives together, okay?"

"Agreed."

"That reminds me. We have to get some sleep because this week will be hectic."

"What do you mean?"

"Our wedding is going to be within the week."

"How?" says Hezekiah. He sits up.

"My dad booked it to take place in the chapel of Central City Church."

Hezekiah chuckles. "I didn't even know that place had a chapel."

"Yeah, I heard it's pretty nice too."

"What does it look like on the inside?"

"According to him, it has a white pulpit with red carpet, light brown walls, bench pews, and a large reception hall. It has a lot of other stuff too, but I'm too tired to remember it all. "

"When did he do this? I thought something like that has to be scheduled months in advance."

"Well, when my father found out that we were a couple, he knew that it was only a matter of time before we got engaged."

"He was right."

Faith yawns. "I'm calling it a night. I'm tired." She scratches her head. "You have a good night, okay?"

"Okay. I love you."

"I love you too. Good night."

"Good night."

Chapter 14

THE BEGINNING
OF SORROWS

THE NEXT DAY, HEZEKIAH GOES TO THEIR NEW
house. The cleaning crew arrives and starts cleaning as he supervises.
He can't shake the funny feeling that the evil spirit who attempted to
attack Faith is only the beginning of what they will have to face.

———————————

At The governor's mansion, the governor's office is overworked. Half
of the staff has called out sick. Working by video conference, Governor
Roxbury talks to Catherine, his lead finance officer.

"Are you sure these numbers are correct?" asks Roxbury.

"Yes, sir. This is exactly how much it will cost to make much-needed
repairs to our city's infrastructure," says Catherine.

Roxbury chuckles. "This is a lot less than I had anticipated. And are we talking about the same city? We are recovering from a massive invasion."

"Yes, sir, the numbers are correct. Remember, those monsters were hunting for people, not so much interested in destroying the city."

"You got a point. However, not to say this lightly, but I did hear about those monsters ripping people out of cars and tearing through homes to get to people. Has all that been covered under the relief plan?"

"Yes, sir. As much as I hate to talk about the invasion, we have to remember that Hezekiah stopped most of the invasion in its tracks. It was a true miracle."

"Yes, it was."

"How is the town hero doing these days?"

"He's getting married soon," says Roxbury.

"Really? It must be to that reporter. Faith, right?"

"Yes. As a matter of fact, we should be receiving an invitation soon. Do you plan to go?"

"Are you asking me out on a date?" asks Catherine, holding her breath.

"I... uh."

"I'm just kidding, sir," she sighs. "I couldn't go, anyway. I feel terrible. My body feels like it's burning up, and I have pain all over."

"Okay. We'll go ahead and cut this meeting short for now. Just get some rest, okay?"

"Okay. we'll video chat tomorrow." Catherine gets up from the computer and collapses to the floor.

"Oh my! Catherine, Catherine! Are you okay?" Roxbury calls the ambulance, and his body tightens. Thoughts of her death swirl through his mind.

Chapter 15

THE BRIDAL STORE

FRANK AND FAITH ENTER THE BRIDAL STORE looking for a dress. The ceiling, drapes, walls, and carpeting are all champagne-colored. Displays of wedding dresses fill the windows. Many windows allow the natural light to shine through the store. Frank's casual attire catches the attention of a saleswoman. His white, short-sleeve-collared shirt, blue slacks, and tan shoes screams, "I need help." Faith's outfit of a white tank dress and white shoes gives the saleswoman some clue as to what the young lady wants.

"Hello. Welcome to Central Bridal. My name is Ms. Hyatt. How may I be of service?"

"We're searching for a bridal gown," says Frank.

"Well, let me show you what we have to offer."

She guides them to dress after dress, but none seem to stand out to Faith. One by one, Faith rejects them. Determined to get a sale, she takes care to keep track of Faith's likes and dislikes, showing her dresses that match her ever-changing preference, to no avail. Faith asks to take a break to look on her own. The saleswoman agrees, makes a few recommendations, and allows for father and daughter to search through the store. The two take a break and sit down across from each other in the lobby.

"What's wrong, Faith? You seem to not be into looking for a dress. What's going on? Are you having second thoughts?" he asks.

"No. Of course not. I have never been so in love with a man before. Every time I see Hezekiah, my mind lights up. There is so much that I could say, but right now, I feel kind of sad."

"Why?"

Faith's throat strains. "Because Mom is not here." A tear trickles down her face. "I know she would be here right now helping me find the most beautiful gown possible. But she's not." Faith rubs her eyes.

Frank gets up and hugs his daughter. She sniffles into her dad's shoulder. He rubs her back.

"I didn't realize this was upsetting to you too," says Frank. "I've been thinking about this the whole time."

Faith lifts her head and rubs her watery eyes. "Really?" she says.

"Yes. I have no doubt she would be here finding a dress and coordinating the entire wedding instead of me. Not that I don't like to do this, but it would have been a joy to see her in action, not only to make your wedding day great but to make up for the unconventional one we had." They let go of each other, and he returns to his chair.

"Really? So, what was your wedding like?" asks Faith, wiping the tears from her eyes.

"Well, oddly enough, it was in the mission field."

"What? I thought that you weren't big on mission trips until you left working at the hospital fulltime."

"You're right, I wasn't. However, your mom and I were excellent friends and had known each other for years. One day, she asked me, out of the blue, to go on a mission trip with her to the Amazon. I had already put in for vacation and had other plans. She insisted that I go. Anyway, we went, and at first, the area was hot and muggy. There were mosquitos everywhere. I was ready to go back home the minute I got to our area. Anyway, after a week of complaining, your mother got tired of it and led me to an isolated area where we were by ourselves. We were on a large rock overlooking the vast jungle at sunset. I never knew nature could be so beautiful. We sat down and started talking. The more we talked, the more I noticed how beautiful your mom was. The way the sunlight radiated through her hair and bounced off her light brown skin made her fascinating to me. What made things better is what happened next."

"What?"

"God said to me, not audibly, of course, that she would be my wife."

"Oh," she says.

"Instead of waiting for another confirmation like any normal person would, the words 'will you marry me' stumbled right out of my mouth."

"What?" Faith chuckles and laughs. "What else happened?" she asks, a smile forming on her face.

"First, her eyes opened wide, and she shook her head in surprise."

"That's understandable. Spring a question like that on someone after just being friends, and you're bound to have a knee-jerk reaction."

"I thought she was going to say no. I was thinking, 'Oh my God, did I mess this up?' As negative thoughts ran through my head and I was getting ready to get up, she said, 'Ask me again.' I was surprised that she said anything at all, let alone 'ask me again.' So, we both stood up, and I got down on one knee and asked her to marry me."

"What did she say?"

Frank chuckles. "She said yes, of course."

"What else happened?"

"Well, as we were traveling back to camp, Maranda told one of the missionary volunteers that I had just proposed to her."

"Okay."

"Well, it turned out that he was a licensed minister and offered to perform the ceremony that evening."

"Wait, what? What are the chances?"

"Your mom looked at me to see if I was going to back out. To both our surprise, I said yes, right then and there. The minister told the people in the area that a wedding was going to take place that night."

"Oh wow, what happened during the ceremony?"

"Oh, the people made a big fuss about it and set up a semi-clear area and even put a makeshift band together in less than an hour. We said, 'I do' under the setting sun in the middle of the Amazon rain forest."

"That sounds so romantic. How come there was no hesitation with Mom? Why did she agree to marry you so fast?"

"Isn't it obvious? My charming, good looks." Frank grins, showing his teeth.

"Dad."

"Okay, okay. I asked your mom that exact question, and she told me that God told her some time ago that I would be her husband. She questioned it at first. However, God kept showing her through countless confirmations that I was the person she should marry. Your mom said that my faith in God, the way I showed kindness to other people who didn't deserve it, the way I defended her when other people tried to talk down to her or take advantage of her, and through many other ways, God proved His word to be correct. In fact, she said God told her to invite me on the trip, and He would prove His word again. She said God told her I would propose to her on that trip."

"What?"

"Yeah. Your mom didn't believe it either, but she decided to have faith and asked me to go. So when I asked her to marry me, she said that her heart nearly jumped out of her chest. Faith, that's why we named you 'Faith' because you are a reminder that God will do what He says He will do; we just got to have faith."

"Wow. Thanks, Dad. I feel a whole lot better now," says Faith, her face brightening.

"Wait, I didn't get to the best part."

"What best part?" asks Faith, narrowing her eyes.

"What happened on our impromptu honeymoon."

"No, Dad, that's quite enough," says Faith. Holding up her hand.

"Oh, it was great! The candles were flickering outside of the hut, and me and your mom—"

"I am not hearing this right now!" Faith covers her ears as her dad playfully tries to tell the story.

Chapter 16

LOYALTY

HEZEKIAH IS AT THE HOUSE, THINKING ABOUT the wedding, how Faith is doing, Frank, and a host of other issues that come to his mind. As he supervises the cleaning crew, the doorbell rings. Wondering if it's another person with the cleaning crew, Hezekiah opens the door. Hezekiah flinches. Julie, Faith's best work friend, is at the door. She is in a red skirt, red jacket, and red pumps. Her red hair, usually styled in a single long braid, is flowing freely across her shoulders and down her back.

"Oh, hey, Julie, how are you doing?"

"I'm doing great, how are you?" says Julie with a playful smile.

Hezekiah rubs the back of his neck. "How do you know about this place?"

"Oh, Faith told me. Can I come in?" she asks with a giggle.

"No, not right now. Faith isn't here."

"Oh, okay. Well, I was wondering if you wanted to do that interview you promised?"

"What interview?"

"You know the one you said you would do before you went to jail," says Julie.

"Oh, right. I completely forgot," says Hezekiah, putting his hand on his head. "However, I'd rather do this at another time. We are completely swamped with cleaning the house."

"Oh, okay." She gazes into Hezekiah's eyes and gently brushes strands of hair off her brow. "You know, I was kind of hoping we could go ahead and do this interview today. It would only take a few minutes. Maybe we could get a cup of coffee and do this interview, or you could come by my office today." She smiles gently.

Is this lady trying to come onto me? "You know what? We're just going to have to wait until Faith and I are both free. Have a good day, Julie," he says as he starts to close the door.

"But wait, I—"

"Have a good day." He closes the door.

Not wanting to take any chances of this story getting out and being twisted out of shape, Hezekiah calls Faith on his phone.

Faith's cell phone rings, and she answers. "Hey, Hezekiah, how are you?"

"Hey. Did you by any chance tell Julie where we are going to live?" asks Hezekiah. Faith raises an eyebrow and plays with her hair. She stands and paces slowly.

"I may have told her about our new place, but why do you ask?" Her voice turns up a squeaky pitch. "What happened?"

"Nothing really. Let's just say that I would rather deal with her with you around."

"Okay," says Faith. Her nostrils flare and her lips curl. "What happened?" she asks with a sharper voice.

Kind of scared now, Hezekiah hesitates to answer. Faith exhales and softens her jaw.

"I'm not mad at you. I'm mad at her. I'm sorry for making it seem like I was blaming you for what may have happened between you two. I know it's not your fault because you were the one who called me to tell me what's going on. So, please, so that I won't be thinking about a million things, tell me what happened."

Relaxing, Hezekiah tells Faith the details of the conversation between Julie and himself, particularly what she was wearing and her body language.

"Am I crazy for thinking that she was coming onto me? Was it just in my head?" asks Hezekiah.

"No. I know women. And I particularly know Julie. I don't know why I told her the address of our new house in the first place." Faith bites her bottom lip. "I'll talk to her tomorrow."

"Okay."

"Also, Hezekiah, you're very special to me... you are very different than other men. I can tell you this without thinking twice because of how much you care about me. I love you. I don't want to be and I'm not going to be the type of woman you are afraid to talk to."

Hezekiah exhales. "Thank you, Faith. I really do appreciate it. I love you too."

Faith hangs up the phone.

"What was that about?" asks Frank.

"It was Julie trying to move in on my man!" shouts Faith. People in the store stop and stare, including Ms. Hyatt. Faith's soft brown eyes widen as she balls her fists.

"Oh no. I see that look in your eyes. Don't do anything rash. I don't want to have to bail you out of jail before your wedding day," says Frank.

"Oh, I'm not going to do anything to her, Dad. We just need to have a conversation."

"So, what happened?"

"She went to the house and tried to ask Hezekiah out on a date. A 'private interview,' she said."

"Oh. I remember that; before the trial, Julie wanted to take Hezekiah out... oh, that's terrible. I can't believe she would still... anyway, I don't want to make matters worse. Just know that you have a great guy who is faithful to you," says Frank.

"You're right, Dad. I'm glad that I do. However, I don't want some woman I thought was my friend try to take Hezekiah away from me. He and I have been through too much together in a short time for me to lose him now."

"You won't lose him. I see him being a very loyal guy for you. Heck, most guys would not even have told their girl what happened. The fact he told you about a potential problem of this kind instead of trying to handle matters on his own shows real maturity."

"I know. A lot of things Hezekiah does are almost unreal. If we didn't have to face up against demonic forces regularly, I would be looking for a 'catch' to Hezekiah's behavior."

"Faith, that is the 'catch,'" says Frank. They both chuckle a little, get up, and continue their shopping at the bridal store.

Chapter 17

CHANCE ENCOUNTER

AN HOUR LATER, THE SALES ASSOCIATE, MS. HYATT, approaches Frank and Faith, who are again sitting down in the same chairs. Assuming Faith has found the dress she wants, Ms. Hyatt approaches. However, the frown on Faiths face tells a different story. Ms. Hyatt walks up as Frank and Faith are in mid-conversation.

"Hey, Ms. Parker, have you found the perfect dress?" asks Ms. Hyatt.

Frank glances at her. "Hello, Ms...."

"Hyatt. It's Ms. Hyatt, sir." She turns her attention back to Faith. "Have you found a dress? From what you told me, your wedding is at the end of this week. We need to find you a dress today."

"I know, but I just don't see a dress that's calling out to me yet," says Faith.

Is it me? Does my breath stink? Is my sales approach lacking in zeal? "Okay, Faith, remember what we talked about? Let's go over what you want."

"Well, I want a sleeveless white dress that goes down to my feet," says Faith.

"Okay, go on."

"I also want it accented with red, or blue, or maybe gold."

Almost blowing a fuse, Ms. Hyatt takes a deep breath and relaxes. "Okay, Ms. Parker, we've been through this before, lets first find the dress, and then we can talk about dress accent colors, okay?"

"Okay." Faith turns toward the window. "Oh, that looks like a nice dress right there."

"Where?" asks Ms. Hyatt, smiling.

Faith points toward the window and sees Julie walking down the street outside the store. Faith's eyes widen.

"Uh oh," says Frank. His daughter jumps out of the chair and runs toward the door.

"Oh, that's a nice dress! Let's try—" Before Ms. Hyatt can get the rest of her sentence out, Faith is rushing out the door.

Ms. Hyatt puts her hand to her face and shakes her head.

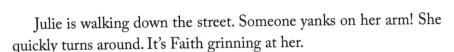

Julie is walking down the street. Someone yanks on her arm! She quickly turns around. It's Faith grinning at her.

"Hey Julie, how are you doing?" says Faith with a squeaky voice.

Julie starts to sweat, and she smiles. "I'm doing great, Faith. How are you?"

"I'm doing good. Julie, I have a question for you."

"Yeah, I'm all ears," she says, voice quivering.

"Can we talk inside?"

"Sure! As long as you let go of my arm," says Julie.

Faith lets go. "I'm sorry, I just got a little carried away there," she says, straightening her dress. Faith and Julie enter the bridal store. Frank gazes at them both and gasps, gets up, and searches for more dresses. Ms. Hyatt wonders what's the cause for alarm. She walks up to Julie and greets her. After she learns the newcomer's name, she is silent. Eavesdropping previously, she goes off to assist another customer.

"That was weird. What was that all about?" asks Julie. Her heartbeat steadily picks up.

"Don't worry about her. Come have a seat," says Faith. They both sit down. Faith takes in a soft steady breath. "I heard you stopped by to see Hezekiah today," she says softly.

Julie's body stiffens, and her eyes slightly widen. "Yes, I talked to Hezekiah today. It was about an interview that we had set up."

"Where were you going to do this interview?"

"I was going to take him to the office."

"Dressed like that? You look very provocative, Julie. How were you going to get there? Was it going to be in your car, or his?"

"Well, at first, I wanted to come in and do the interview. But since he said that you weren't home, I offered to go to the office to conduct the interview there."

"So, let me get this straight," says Faith with a pleasant sternness. Julie's mouth goes dry. "You were going to conduct an interview in my house, dressed in a red miniskirt, to a man I'm about to marry on Friday!?" shouts Faith.

Julie jumps up out of her chair. "Now wait a minute, Faith. What are you trying to say? I'm not a slut. And I'm certainly no home wrecker. You can keep your judgmental comments to yourself!"

"Julie, don't pretend! You're talking to me," says Faith. She slowly stands. "We've been friends and colleagues for a long time. I know your history."

Julie tries to think of something to say. They've been out together too many times as friends and reporters for her to try to trick Faith. There was a time where Faith would see Julie with a different man almost every two weeks. In fact, on one of those occasions, Faith had to save Julie from an abusive man who found out she was cheating on him with another guy. So, Julie takes a deep breath and sits down. Both ladies are silent.

"Faith... I'm sorry. I won't do it again, okay?" says Julie. Putting her hands up in surrender, "I just wanted to see If I..."

"'If' what? If you had a shot with my man?"

"Look, Faith. I'm sorry. I won't do it again, okay? Next time, I'll just be professional when I see Hezekiah."

"Stay away from Hezekiah!"

Everyone in the bridal shop stops to stare. The two ladies are silent. Julie glances at Faith's fists.

"Okay, I can do that too," says Julie.

"Good," says Faith. "I'm glad that we've reached an understanding," says Faith. She straightens her dress.

"Me too," says Julie. She wipes her brow from sweat. Are we still friends?"

"Sure, just as long as you stay away from Hezekiah."

"Okay."

Julie gets up and speed walks out of the shop.

Ms. Hyatt comes back and approaches Faith. "I can't believe I've been such an idiot," says Ms. Hyatt. Slapping her palm against her forehead.

"What do you mean?" asks Faith.

"Your marrying Hezekiah. King Hezekiah, the Spirit Warrior," says Ms. Hyatt.

Faith frowns her face.

"Have I got a dress for you," says Ms. Hyatt.

Chapter 18

LOVE UNREALIZED

WORRIED ABOUT CATHERINE, GOVERNOR Roxbury calls an ambulance to check on her. The paramedics drive her to the hospital. Governor Roxbury arranges for his limo driver to take him to the hospital where she is staying. While traveling to the hospital, he recalls all of the memories he has with Catherine, all the times they laughed and cried together. He hopes he has more time with her.

The governor waits in the brightly lit waiting room, surrounded by his security detail. He's on pins and needles while waiting on news from the doctors. He taps his fingers on the smooth wooden armrest of his chair and checks his watch. His security detail notices a doctor headed their way. The doctor asks permission to pass through the security detail. Roxbury nods, and the doctor is let in.

"Governor Roxbury, I'm surprised to see you here," says Dr. Jakes.

"Yes, I wanted to check on Catherine. How is she doing?" He asks, tapping his foot.

"I'm afraid it's not looking good."

"What do you mean?" Roxbury asks. He stands up.

"Whatever she contracted is causing her nervous system to shut down slowly," says Jakes. Roxbury frowns.

"Is there anything you can do for it?"

"We have to run more tests to find out exactly what kind of sickness this is. Until then, the best thing we can do is treat her symptoms."

"Is there any way I can see her?"

"Yes, you can. However, you have to put on PPE because she could be highly contagious. In fact, walk with me, and I'll take you to a room where you can put on some of our scrubs and equipment."

Governor Roxbury and his security staff follow the doctor to a private room. Roxbury and the doctor put on the PPE, then go to Catherine's room. The governor and doctor go in, and the security detail stays at the door.

"Okay. Thank you very much, doctor," says Roxbury.

"Let me know if you need anything," says the doctor, and he walks off.

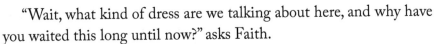

"Wait, what kind of dress are we talking about here, and why have you waited this long until now?" asks Faith.

"Well, this dress is expensive," says Ms. Hyatt.

"You do know that my dad is a doctor, right?"

"It's not just that; this dress is a part of my private collection that I only share with my high-end clients. You know, movie stars and the like."

"Again, why are you sharing this with us now?" asks Faith.

"Because of what Hezekiah did for me," says Ms. Hyatt, smiling.

Frank nervously asks, "What did Hezekiah do for you?"

"It was during the invasion."

"Oh, okay," Frank wipes his brow, and Faith lightly punches his arm. "What happened?" he asks.

"When the evacuation order was given, I chose to stay home. I didn't want to go inside of that bunker the governor was talking about. I figured that if I was going to die, I would want to die in my own house and not in a bunker. Huge mistake. Anyway, I was in my house, and a red monster broke into my house and chased me. I ran outside into a dimly lit back alley to get away, and I saw my own shadow come up from the ground and turn into a devil!"

"Oh my, what happened next?"

"It opened its mouth to eat me. But Hezekiah came from nowhere and sliced straight through the demon and ran off."

"Wow. What happened to the demon that chased you outside in the first place?" asks Faith.

"It ran outside, but instead of coming after me, it chased Hezekiah."

"Oh wow," says Frank. He glances at Faith.

"That's why I need to show you this dress because if it weren't for your groom, I would have been doomed."

Ms. Hyatt takes them to the back to a room full of custom-made dresses. Faith's jaw drops. She puts her hand over her mouth. "These dresses are beautiful," says Faith. She rushes to look through the gowns; each one is more beautiful than the next.

"This is the dress I wanted to show you right here." Ms. Hyatt takes them to the center of the room and pulls a sheet off of a dress on a display stand. Faith's eyes widen at its appearance in the light. It's a sleeveless white dress made of silk accented with gold.

"I've got to get this dress," says Faith jumping up and down.

"We'll take it. How much?" asks Frank.

"It's on me," says Ms. Hyatt.

"What? No, we can't do that," says Frank. "How much, for real?"

"It's really no problem. I'll write it off on my taxes. Besides, I promised God during the invasion that if He got me out alive, I would do something to show my gratitude. Well, with Hezekiah saving me and all, and you marrying him, I thought this would be the perfect time to bless God by blessing His people."

Frank looks up with his hands clasped. "My God, You are so awesome."

Faith and Frank finish things at the bridal store and prepare to leave. As they step out the door, Ms. Hyatt grabs Frank's hand softly, looks into his eyes, and smiles.

"Make sure you thank Hezekiah for me," says Ms. Hyatt. Frank smiles back.

"I'll tell you what, if you come to the wedding with us, we can introduce you," says Frank.

"Really? Where will the wedding take place?"

"Central City Church," says Frank. "Be our guest. We would love to have you."

"In that case, I'll see you on Friday!"

"Yeah, see you on Friday," says Frank as they leave the bridal store.

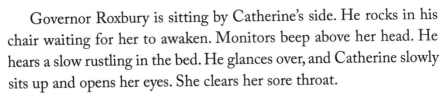

Governor Roxbury is sitting by Catherine's side. He rocks in his chair waiting for her to awaken. Monitors beep above her head. He hears a slow rustling in the bed. He glances over, and Catherine slowly sits up and opens her eyes. She clears her sore throat.

"Hey," says Catharine softly.

"Hey, yourself. How are you holding up?" asks the governor.

"I don't feel too good. If it wasn't for the medicine they're giving me for pain, I would feel a lot worse." She notices he's sitting close to her. "You shouldn't be this close to me. I could be highly contagious."

"I don't care," says Roxbury. He moves closer to her and holds her hand.

"Aren't you worried about what the press might think if they see you in here with me like this?"

"I don't care, Catherine. I don't want to be distant from you anymore. If I have to, I will resign and do something else," says Roxbury.

"No. I can't let you do that. We need you as governor. If anything, I'll quit first before I let you resign. However, I'm afraid that I don't have that long." Catherine coughs.

"What are you talking about? Don't talk like that!"

"I wish we had more time, but I'm just glad that we could be here together at this moment. I'm also glad I was there by your side for you all these years when you needed me. Even though we were never lovers the way we wanted to be, it was still nice just being with you. I'm sad now because I'll have to wait for you."

"Wait for me, why?"

"Because I have to wait for you in heaven." Catherine's eyes roll to the back of her head and she shakes violently. Her monitors buzz and ring.

A slew of medical personnel rush into Catherine's room and rush the governor out. Roxbury waits in the cold hallway, hoping for the best.

After fifteen minutes, Dr. Jakes exits and talks to him. Governor Roxbury silently weeps. He puts his hand over his face. Catherine, the love that could have been, has died.

Chapter 19

COLD FEET

IT'S FRIDAY. AFTER A WEEK OF PREPARATION AND a barrage of phone calls, the wedding is set to begin. Frank arranges for Faith's Jeep to be dropped off at her new house. Hezekiah makes some phone calls to the City of Light, inviting people to the wedding. No one can come. On the other hand, Faith arranges for her family and friends to be at the wedding despite the short notice. She even pulls together a wedding party and gets Julie to be a bridesmaid.

Almost all the guests are in attendance. Faith is in her bridal chamber, talking to her father. The walls and curtains are pristine white with navy blue carpet.

"I can't believe this day is finally here!" says Faith, smiling wide. Her hands tremble. "I can't believe that Hezekiah and I are going to be married!"

"I'm happy for you, dear," says Frank. They both smile from ear to ear. "If it were any other guy, I would ask if you were ready for this. However, since Hezekiah risked his life not only for you but for the both of us, so many times, other than the Messiah, I couldn't think of a better man who loves you more."

"I know. I'm just so happy. I know that neither one of us is perfect. I just don't want to mess this up. What if when we get married, everything changes between us? What if somehow he or I get tempted by another person and fail? What if I stop loving him because we get too familiar with each other? What if one of us dies? What if—"

Frank puts his hand up. "Faith, there is no doubt that Satan will attack you. But just remember that God is the one who is more powerful than any devil. Life will throw curveball after curveball, but just lean into God to get you both through the strikeouts in life, so you can both hit a home run for the Lord together."

"What?"

"You know, baseball."

"Dad..." Faith starts to chuckle, then bursts out in laughter.

"What? I thought that the baseball analogy was pretty good," says Frank, smiling.

"Yeah, Dad, but not everyone would understand that. Not only that, but you're also a doctor, not a baseball player."

"So, I may have hit a few home runs when I was a kid," says Frank.

"Really, Dad," says Faith, raising an eye brow and grinning.

"No, but still, I could have."

Faith bursts out laughing.

"Okay, seriously, when you feel like your marriage is under attack, don't turn to a girlfriend who will tell you to leave him. Don't turn to another man and tell him your problems with Hezekiah. Turn to the Lord because He is the only one who will not only listen but help you solve any problem between you two, as long as you are willing. Also, like I was saying before, when life sends your marriage storm after storm, lean into God; He will get you both through. I believe the Bible says in Psalm 91: 'Whoever dwells in the shelter of the Most High will rest in the shadow of the Almighty.' Put your marriage in God's hands, and He will make sure to prosper you."

"Okay, Dad, I feel better now. That kind of took the edge off, especially about the whole strike-out thing," says Faith, face red. She chuckles again.

"Okay, Faith," says Frank, grinning.

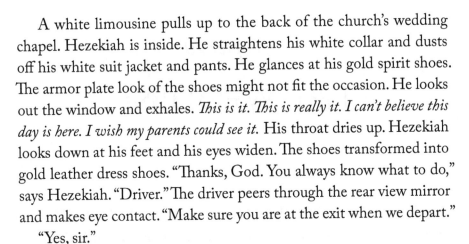

A white limousine pulls up to the back of the church's wedding chapel. Hezekiah is inside. He straightens his white collar and dusts off his white suit jacket and pants. He glances at his gold spirit shoes. The armor plate look of the shoes might not fit the occasion. He looks out the window and exhales. *This is it. This is really it. I can't believe this day is here. I wish my parents could see it.* His throat dries up. Hezekiah looks down at his feet and his eyes widen. The shoes transformed into gold leather dress shoes. "Thanks, God. You always know what to do," says Hezekiah. "Driver." The driver peers through the rear view mirror and makes eye contact. "Make sure you are at the exit when we depart."

"Yes, sir."

Hezekiah opens the door and steps out of the limo. He takes in a breath. The sun shines through the crystal blue sky, and the birds tweet. It's a beautiful day for a wedding. He takes a step, and his hand trembles. He balls his fist and shakes his hand. "I hope I'm not putting Faith in danger."

Be strong and courageous. Do not be afraid; do not be discouraged, for the Lord your God will be with you wherever you go. He who finds a wife finds what is good and receives favor from the Lord.

"Thank You, God." Hezekiah walks into the back entrance.

Chapter 20

THE WEDDING

TWENTY MINUTES LATER, THE WEDDING IS SET TO begin. Guests pack the church chapel. Everyone Faith invited has shown up except for the governor and some of his staff. People are chatting about the wedding. In two different locations, Hezekiah and Faith get themselves prepared. The wedding coordinators, Dr. Scott and Ms. Amy, take care of different functions, such as seating people and the food arrangement. The pastor, dressed in a white robe with a red collar, takes the stage and prepares to speak.

"Ladies and gentlemen, without further ado, the wedding is about to start. So please, everyone, if you're not already seated, take a seat."

The violinist starts to play.

"I want to say a quick prayer before we start. So, everyone, bow your heads and close your eyes. Dear God, we thank You for today. We thank You for the glorious union between Faith and Hezekiah. We pray as the two become one that You make their marriage a shining example of Your love. We pray this in Jesus's name, amen," says Pastor Brian.

He remains standing as the music starts to play. Hezekiah and the groomsmen come out of the side entrance and stand in their places. His crisp white suit glows under the church lights. He gazes toward the door, silently waiting for Faith, his bride, to come forth. Down the aisle, the door opens. A group of little children run out with banners and tambourines, laughing and saying, "The bride is coming, the bride is coming."

Everyone stares at the doorway. Lights shine on the doorway, and Faith emerges. Everyone's jaws drop. Her silk white dress shines and sparkles in the light. Frank is dressed in white and gold. His suit shines brightly, but Faith clearly steals the show. Faith and her father walk down the aisle. Through her veil, she gazes at Hezekiah and smiles. Faith and Frank reach the base of the stairs leading to the altar. Frank kisses her, smoothly guides her up the stairs, places her hand in Hezekiah's hand, and quietly backs away. Faith and Hezekiah hold hands. They peer into each other's eyes. The pastor starts to speak.

"Dearly beloved, we are gathered here today to join these two in holy matrimony. If anyone objects to this union, speak now or forever hold your peace." No one says a word. "Marriage is a picture of what Christ has done for the church. His sacrifice on the Cross has washed our sins. As the bride of Christ, we are washed from our sins. Although our sins were as red as scarlet, now the record is as white as snow. Your record before God can be clean too. I want everyone to bow your heads and close your eyes. If anyone wants to receive Jesus Christ as Lord and Savior, raise your hands." To the pastor's surprise, a few people put their hands in the air. "Repeat after me: Dear Jesus, I believe that You are the Son of God and You died on the Cross to save me from my sins. I also believe that You rose from the dead as proof of who You are. Lord Jesus, Forgive me of my sins. I accept You into my heart as Lord and Savior." A few people accepted Jesus, much to the pastor's surprise.

Everyone opens their eyes, and the pastor has a gold communion cup and some bread.

"This is for believers only. Anyone who is a new creation in Christ can take part, but for today, it will be for the bride and groom."

The pastor gives Hezekiah and Faith the bread and grape juice.

"The night that Jesus was to suffer and die, He celebrated Passover with His disciples. He said to them: 'Take and eat; this is My body which was broken for you.' Then He took a cup, and when He had given thanks, He gave it to them, saying, 'Drink from it, all of you. This is My blood of the covenant, which is poured out for many for the forgiveness of sins.' Let us take Communion together."

Hezekiah and Faith feed each other the sacraments.

"Communion is a symbol of the covenant that God has made with His bride. It is also the symbol of unity in this marriage taking place today." The pastor looks at Faith and asks, "Faith Parker, do you take Hezekiah to be your lawfully wedded husband? Through sickness and health, for richer and poorer, as long as you both may live?"

"I do," says Faith.

"Hezekiah, do you take Faith Parker to be your lawfully wedded wife? Through sickness and health, for richer and poorer, as long as you both may live?"

"I do," says Hezekiah.

"By the power vested in me by God, I pronounce you husband and wife. Hezekiah, you may kiss your bride."

Hezekiah lifts the veil and gazes into Faith's chocolate-colored eyes. His pulse races. Faith peers into his. Her heart hammers into her chest. For a moment, they pause. Hezekiah gently places his palm on her face. Electricity moves from her face into his hand and across his arm, into his chest. Hezekiah moves his head closer. Faith tilts her head and moves it closer. Her lips reach his and connect; her lips tingle. The warmth expands into her head, chest, and flutters in her stomach. Hezekiah's heart races. Warmth rushes and expands through his body. Faith raises to her toes as Hezekiah reaches with his other arm and holds her. The crowd bursts into applause. Faith and Hezekiah pull away slightly, smiling.

The crowd quiets down. "Now, may I introduce to you Mr. and Mrs. Hezekiah Jaxon?" says the pastor. The crowd applauds. The newly married couple release from their embrace and wave to the gathering.

"Now may our reception begin," says the pastor. The murmuring audience gets up and heads for the door.

The photographer sets up his photo equipment. The guests slowly file out of the room.

The photographer arranges the wedding party and starts taking pictures. He takes pictures of the bride and her bridesmaids, the groom and his groomsmen, the bridesmaids with the groomsmen, the pastor and the groomsman, the pastor's wife and the bridesmaids. He starts taking pictures of the bride and groom. He tells Faith to lean closer to Hezekiah. She whispers something to Hezekiah, and his eyes widen.

"Okay, now get behind her and put your arms around her waist," says the photographer. "Hezekiah, don't move."

Hezekiah puts his arms around her waist.

"Okay now, Faith, lean in closer."

Faith leans into Hezekiah.

"Oh no. I've run out of storage; let me load another memory card. It will just take a second," says the photographer.

During the technical pause, Faith whispers in his ear. "You know what I've said before. I've been waiting for this day for my whole short life. Not only so I could marry the man of my dreams, but so that my inner desire could be satisfied."

Hezekiah's jaw drops. "What?" says Hezekiah softly. He starts to fan his face.

"I've been super good. I have never let another man touch me inappropriately throughout high school and college, even when I wanted them to. When we started dating, it got even harder to resist you. You did your part in keeping pure because of the man you are, and I'm glad. Now, however, your responsibility has changed. In the same way that you were strong enough to resist me, you need to find the quickest way out of here so that we can become one," says Faith. She moves her head close to his face, lightly kisses his cheek, and pulls back. Hezekiah exhales. His heart pounds in his chest. A natural desire he has for Faith swells in his chest. Now that they are married, there is no need to keep emotions at bay.

"Okay," says the photographer. "Now, let's get started. Now, Hezekiah, place your chin on her neck and put your face against hers." Hezekiah moves his face a hair length away from Faith's. The light touch sends a gentle shock to his face and neck. They both smile for the camera, and the photographer starts to count down from five.

"Remember what I said," whispers Faith.

Chapter 21

THE RECEPTION

PEOPLE TAKE THEIR SEATS IN THE RECEPTION HALL. After taking pictures, Frank leaves the wedding party and enters the reception hall. Tearing up, he sits at his table alone thinking about the beautiful moments he and Faith shared. Some old work associates come up and congratulate Frank on landing Hezekiah for a son-in-law. They talk, and he slightly turns his head. A gorgeous woman dressed in light purple sits across from him.

Who is that? The lady glances at Frank and smiles. Frank's work associates leave the table. The lady leaves her table and strolls toward him. Frank leans back and takes in a breath.

"Dr. Parker, it's good to see you," says the woman.

Frank blinks his eyes. "What, do I know you?"

"You don't recognize me?" She smiles. "It's Ms. Hyatt from the bridal store."

Frank's eyes widen. "Oh, I didn't know it was you. You look gorgeous."

"Thanks." She flicks a few strands of hair away from her face. She blinks and frowns. "Wait, how did I look before?"

"You looked good before, but you look even better now," says Frank.

"You don't look too bad yourself," says Ms. Hyatt smirking.

"Thanks. I keep myself looking sharp."

"I'm grateful that you invited me. This is a spectacular event."

"I'm glad that you came. Who have you seen so far?" asks Frank. Ms. Hyatt takes a chair and sits.

"Well, to be honest, I wanted to get a chance to meet the governor, but I guess he's tied up in something important. Not that this wedding is not important, but he may be tied up in some situation."

"Don't worry, I understand."

"If you don't mind me asking, how are you holding up?"

"What do you mean?"

"Well, your only daughter got married today. And your wife is not here. I thought maybe..."

Frank stands and lifts his palms chest level. "Ms. Hyatt, I'm glad you came, but I can't talk about this right now." He turns around and walks. Someone softly grabs his hand. A tingling travels from his hand into his forearm. He stops and turns his head. It's Ms. Hyatt.

"Dr. Parker, I'm sorry. Please don't leave. Please stay."

"Why?"

"I didn't come with anyone, and you're the only person I really know here. And even then, it's not that well. I'm sorry to pry," says Ms. Hyatt. Frank exhales, and they stroll to their table.

Frank sits, and Ms. Hyatt sits across the table. "I'm sorry, Ms. Hyatt, but to this day, the topic of my late wife saddens me."

"Okay. I understand. Changing the subject, what kind of medical work do you practice? You mentioned previously that you are a medical doctor."

"Yes, I'm a missionary doctor."

"What does that entail?"

"I treat people that the regular hospital would not treat, like the poor or dangerous. And I get paid from the hospital through one of their networks."

"That's actually very interesting. What was your last patient like?"

"Well, my last patient was Hezekiah."

"No way! How did that happen?"

"Well, one day, we were in the desert because we were on our way back from visiting someone. Faith looked over and noticed a body in the middle of the desert. Keep in mind, the body was some distance from the road, so it was a miracle she spotted him. Anyway, we pulled up in our Jeep. Hezekiah was a complete mess. He was unconscious, lying in a pool of his own blood."

Ms. Hyatt frowns.

"Anyway, convinced he was dead, I thought that we should leave, but she insisted we help him. So, we stopped the bleeding, bandaged him up, and brought him back home."

"My goodness. What happened next? And how long did it take for you to figure out that he was right for your daughter?"

"Good question. Well, at first, I didn't like him."

"Why?"

"Because I walked into his room one day, and he and my daughter looked like they had a real connection."

"In what way?"

"While she was feeding him, they were smiling and giggling with each other. Sometime after that, I wanted to find out more about him, and I did. I thought I did anyway. Through some arm twisting, and much questioning, I thought I found out that he killed my wife. You know about the whole trial thing, right?"

"Yeah, I do; where everyone thought he was responsible for the death of your... anyway, everyone knows about the trial."

"I hated him at first for it," says Frank. The reception hall erupts into applause. Frank and Ms. Hyatt turn toward the chapel hallway.

The wedding party comes out. Frank and Ms. Hyatt stand. Everyone stands and applauds. The happy couple smile and wave as people take pictures.

———————————◦———————————

The pastor walks out and takes a microphone. "Dear God, we thank You for this day, and we pray that You bless the food. We pray that You bless this couple with a joyful union. In Jesus's name, amen."

As both Hezekiah and Faith lift their heads from prayer, Ms. Hyatt and Frank pull chairs to the wedding party's table. Ms. Hyatt sits next to Faith, and Frank sits next to Hezekiah.

Chapter 22

THE RECEPTION: PART 2

"HEY, YOU TWO! HOW ARE YOU DOING?" ASKS MS. Hyatt.

"We're doing well, Ms. Hyatt. How are you?" asks Faith.

Hezekiah smiles and nods.

"Frank, can you continue your story?" Ms. Hyatt asks.

"Yes. From my perspective, when I thought that Hezekiah killed my wife, I hated him until he saved my daughter the first two times," says Frank.

Caught off guard by the topic, both Hezekiah and Faith sharpen their attention.

"Really? Do tell," says Ms. Hyatt.

"Well, the first time Hezekiah saved Faith was when she was confronted by criminals who wanted revenge. In the past, she did a story that uncovered a drug ring in the City of Light. The criminals were arrested but escaped police custody to kill Faith. After Hezekiah saved her, I was grateful. However, it wasn't until he saved her from the attack on Phoenicia that I completely forgave him for what I thought that he did."

"Faith, what changed your mind about Hezekiah? And how did you feel when he saved you?"

"The first time he saved me, I still hated him, but something chipped away at my heart when he saved me from those men. The second time he saved me on Phoenicia, my heart was in a state of confusion because so much happened that day. Warlord had just killed my friends and my mentor, Ms. Collins." Faith wipes a tear from her eye. Hezekiah puts his arm around her, and warmth cascades into her body. "Anyway, when he saved me from Warlord, I was grateful, and part of me started to fall for Hezekiah, but after the moment was over, my infatuation was overpowered by hatred."

"What happened? What was the turning point for you and Hezekiah?"

"When I forgave him for what I thought he did," says Faith.

"What prompted this?"

"Hezekiah's death," says Faith.

Ms. Hyatt leans back in her chair. "What? How on earth did this happen?" asks Ms. Hyatt.

"He was fighting another version of Warlord. Warlord found me in the pharmacy by our house and attacked me. He chased my dad and me out of the pharmacy, and tried to kill me. Hezekiah came out of nowhere and fought him. Mind you, Hezekiah was still recovering from his first encounter with Warlord. When he came to our rescue this time, it was very unexpected. Anyway, in the course of the fight, Hezekiah was stabbed."

"Oh, my goodness," says Ms. Hyatt. She moves her palm over her mouth.

"Of course, we were able to bring him back to life. However, before we did, I remember hearing the question in my head, 'Is this what you wanted?' I felt so guilty that I couldn't get past it. During that moment, God dealt with me and wanted me to forgive him. When I forgave him and let go of the hurt, love for him started to grow. At first, I thought it was just friendship, but it kept growing the more time I spent with him. Even when I hated myself for it, love grew more. The day we found out he was not responsible for my mother's death, my love manifested without hindrance. When we kissed for the first time, my love for him soared to new heights."

"Hezekiah, how do you feel about all of this?"

He thinks for a moment about the experiences they've been through so far and how their love for each other has strengthened. "I'm just grateful to God for giving me Faith. She is everything I want in a woman and more. There is no one I would rather be with. I don't know what I would do if I lost her." He smiles at Faith.

"Well, let's not worry about anything like that right now," says Faith. The waiters passes out the food.

"Ms. Hyatt, is there anyone special in your life right now?" asks Faith.

"No, not right now. I've actually never been married."

"Really?" asks Frank. "You own a bridal store and never been married?"

"Yeah, I could never find the right person. This is why I put all of my passions into dressmaking."

"Interesting," says Frank.

"Oh, I nearly forgot. Hezekiah, I wanted to thank you for what you've done for me," says Ms. Hyatt.

"Wait, what do you mean? I just met you today."

Faith taps him. "You saved her during the invasion," says Faith.

"I did?"

"Yes, you did," says Ms. Hyatt. "I was running out of my house, and I was stopped by a demon. You came out of nowhere and sliced straight through it and kept going throughout the city. What was going through your head that night?"

"That night, before I got to the city, I thought everyone died because I saw some of the city in flames. I was in sorrow. God reassured me and kept me going. However, that didn't stop me from being angry. I was pissed when I charged into the city. I struck down every demon I saw as I made my way to the crown, the Helmet of Salvation, to save the city."

"Wait, I don't think we ever talked about this. How did you get the crown?" says Faith.

"Remember when you and your father took me on the city tour?"

"Yes," says Faith.

"On the last part of the tour, you two took me to a mysterious statue at the entrance of the city."

"Yeah. The mysterious statue of the armored king on a rearing horse," says Frank.

"Oh, the statue of the king," says Ms. Hyatt. "The legend states that the statue of the king appeared overnight. No one knows where it came from. It also has an inscription on the statue: 'When the sky gets dark, and the enemy comes in like a flood, a champion will arise and lead the city to victory.' Some say that it's a symbol for strong political leadership in the city. However, having lived through the invasion, I'm pretty sure that inscription on the statue was about Hezekiah."

"Yes, it was," says Frank.

Hezekiah scratches his head. "I don't want to take praise away from God here. He saved the city. I was just the instrument He used. Anyway, remember the golden crown on top of the king's head?

"Yes," says Faith.

"The Helmet of Salvation was the golden crown on the king's head."

"Oh!" says Frank and Faith.

"That was so obvious," says Faith.

"When I got that final piece of the armor, I was able to save the city from the invasion.

"What did the full armor look like, and how did it feel?" asks Faith.

"Well, I couldn't see myself in the armor, but the power difference was significant. As powerful as the other parts are individually, it's nothing compared to when they are all put together. It's like going from a tank to a battleship. It's quite powerful. Not only that, but the sword also became so powerful that the slightest swing caused a massive shockwave of fire. The power-up continued for the entire fight with Warlord's army."

"Wow," says Frank.

Hezekiah glances around the room. "Hey, where is the governor? He was supposed to be the guest of honor."

"I don't know. I haven't heard from him all morning," says Frank. "I left several messages, but he's just not answering the phone. I hope something bad didn't happen."

"That's the last thing we want around here," says Hezekiah.

"Well, maybe he's just late or his schedule clashed with today. I don't know, but I do know he wanted to be here," says Frank.

"Faith, where do you plan on going for the honeymoon?" asks Ms. Hyatt.

"Well, we haven't really thought about it. The wedding came so fast that we didn't really have time to think about it," says Faith.

"So, what do you plan to do after this?"

"I don't know," she says.

"We'll think of somewhere to go," says Hezekiah. "Oh, maybe we can go to the beach for our honeymoon. The City of Light has a great beach. White, warm sand between our toes sounds nice."

Faith glances at him. "Yes, that does sound nice," says Faith, rubbing his leg. "We could also go to the woods and explore the great outdoors. There is a nice cabin in the mountains that I've been looking at."

"Oh, okay. It sounds like you two have got some ideas," says Frank, knowing full well what his daughter's plans are.

A few minutes later, as people are eating, the disk jockey plays dance music. Faith gets Hezekiah's attention, looks straight into his eyes, and gently slides her hand across his leg.

I have got to get us out of here, thinks Hezekiah. "You're having fun, aren't you?"

"Yep," says Faith. We can have even more fun as soon as we get out of here," she says, licking her lips.

Hezekiah is about to rush them out until Julie waves at Faith. The distraction frustrates them both.

"Faith, they expect you to throw the bouquet, dance with your husband, your father, and they expect Hezekiah to throw the garter."

"For what?" says Faith sternly.

"I don't know. I don't go to weddings often."

Faith exhales. "I'm sorry, Julie. Where do we go?"

Chapter 23

AFFECTION & ATTRACTION

MINUTES LATER, FAITH GETS READY TO THROW the bridal bouquet. All the single women gather around. She throws the bouquet, and Ms. Hyatt catches it. "My word," she says. The other women cheer and clap. Minutes later, Hezekiah removes the garter from Faith's leg and throws it into the crowd of single men. The men gasp, and it flies past them. It lands in Frank's lap. He glances around. The men in the room hoot and clap.

The wedding coordinator, Ms. Amy, announces that the father-daughter dance is about to start, and the music begins to play. Frank walks over to Faith, chuckling. Faith narrows her eyes.

Frank smiles. "May I have this dance?" asks Frank. He extends his hand.

"Sure," says Faith. She grabs his hand, and a smirk appears on his face. *What is he up to?*

They go to the center of the room. Slow music plays, and they sway to the music. Frank chuckles a little.

"What is it? What's so funny?" asks Faith, narrowing her eyes.

"The way you and Hezekiah are behaving."

"What do you mean?"

"You two are so love-struck that you can't wait to get out of here," says Frank. Faith gasps and stiffens. Her cheeks flush, and she lowers her head. They sway silently for a moment. "Is it that obvious?" she says softly.

"Not to everyone else."

"Is that a bad thing?"

"Heck no. That's how your mom and I were. She used to always steal me away just to kiss me. And I always did the same thing. In fact, there was one time, on a mission trip, we were in the middle of the woods, separated from our fellow travelers. The villagers in that particular village didn't want to hear the gospel, so they attacked us. We fled for our lives."

"Wow, I didn't realize you were in danger more than once," says Faith.

"Many times, Faith, we had to face danger. Anyway, we were a good distance away from all the upheaval, and luckily, I still had the camping supplies with me. It was sunset, and the sun was setting fairly quickly. It looked like we were going to spend the night there, so I pitched a tent. The temperature outside started to drop and we went inside to lie down. Then your mom heard a sound in the trees. I told her to hide. I went outside to see what was coming."

"What happened?"

"We were followed. The rumbling in the trees came closer and closer," says Frank.

"What did you do?"

"I picked up a stick and stood my ground to see what it would be, and finally, it charged out."

"What was it?"

"It was a fawn being chased by another fawn. I was happily surprised. Anyway, I got back into the tent because it was cold. I went to hold her. She said, 'You are so stupid to do that. Why did you do that?' I told her, 'I don't know. I just wanted to protect you.' She said, 'Please don't do that again. I could have lost you.' She kissed me. I kissed her back. We didn't stop kissing, and got under the covers. Your mom needed to make sure I really wasn't hurt, and one thing led to another..."

Faith clears her throat. "Anyway, that was the night you were conceived. Nine months later, she gave birth to a beautiful baby girl. Affection and physical desire are both essential in a relationship. They're the grease in the wheels of a marriage. If you two can't enjoy each other's company in that way, it makes for a very dull union. You two genuinely love each other, so affection is a good thing; don't ever be embarrassed by it."

The music stops, and the people applaud. The announcer calls for the bride and groom to dance. Hezekiah joins her as Frank walks off. Hezekiah and Faith start to dance. They sway silently for a moment.

"I notice you and your dad were in deep conversation. Is everything okay?"

"Yeah, everything is great. He just told me quite a story about how I was conceived."

"Oh."

"I didn't let him finish, though."

"Okay."

"He just reaffirmed to me that affection and attraction are excellent in marriage. It's not something to be embarrassed about," says Faith.

"He's a wise man. I'm glad that he's your dad and not someone else."

"I'm glad too. I'm glad I got two fathers who love me, One up above and one down here. You know, some say that a father's love is supposed to be an example of how God's love is toward us."

"I can see why people say that," says Hezekiah. Faith gazes into his eyes and smiles.

"You know, the Bible says, in Song of Solomon 1:1-4, 'let him kiss me with the kisses of his mouth—for your love is more delightful than wine. Pleasing is the fragrance of your perfumes; your name is like perfume poured out. No wonder the young women love you! Take me away with you—let us hurry! Let the king bring me into his chambers,'" says Faith.

"It also says in Song of Solomon, chapter 2 verse 14: 'My dove in the clefts of the rock, in the hiding places on the mountainside, show me your face, let me hear your voice; for your voice is sweet, and your face is lovely,'" says Hezekiah. "You are so beautiful, inside and out, and there is no one I would rather be with. Don't worry, I'll get us out of here soon."

He gives her a soft kiss on the lips and pulls back. Faith kisses him and the crowd whistles, hoots, and applauds. Hezekiah and Faith stop kissing and swaying.

"I forgot where we were for a second there," says Hezekiah.

"I did too," she says.

They stop dancing, and the music changes. Hezekiah claps her hand and leads her toward the edge of the dance floor. "Ha. Here is our chance to escape," says Hezekiah. But the announcer invites the people who caught the bouquet and the garter to come out and dance.

"Didn't your dad catch the garter?" asks Hezekiah.

"Yeah, he did. Who caught the bouquet?"

They both think about it for a second. "Ms. Hyatt," they say in unison. "We can't leave now," says Faith.

Frank glances across at Ms. Hyatt sitting next to him and says, "May I have this dance?"

"Sure," says Ms. Hyatt.

The two get up, walk to the dance floor, and dance. Frank is sweating.

"Feeling nervous, Dr. Parker?"

"I haven't really danced with a woman other than my daughter in a long time. Am I doing okay?"

"Of course. You're just fine. You may be a bit rusty, but you're doing just fine," says Ms. Hyatt.

"Okay, maybe I'm out of practice. If you're interested, maybe you can help me out with that?"

"What do you have in mind?"

"I was thinking we could go dancing next weekend? That is, if you're available."

Ms. Hyatt grins. "I would be delighted."

"I'm sorry, Ms. Hyatt, I forgot to ask you, what is your first name?"

"Marie."

"Marie?" he says, raising an eye brow. "That's a nice name," says Frank thinking about his wife Maranda.

The music ends, and Hezekiah and Faith attempt to slip out, but the announcer invites everyone to the dance floor. The sudden influx of people forces Hezekiah and Faith onto the dance floor again. They sigh. The music leads everyone into a shuffle. After a short while, they move to the music. Faith notices that Hezekiah can't do this particular dance step. She shows him slowly, and he starts to learn the steps.

Hezekiah starts to make the dance moves into his own, and Faith laughs. They both dance together, getting in sync with each other's moves and spins. They are the center of attention, stealing the show. Frank shakes off the rust from his moves and puts on a show. Marie outshines him as she adds even more intention to her dance steps. The crowd hoots as they see Marie dance. Everyone laughs and has a good time.

The music stops, and the wedding coordinators grab Faith's hand, gets Hezekiah's attention, and motions for them to follow her. The groomsmen and bridesmaids follow.

"Okay, guests," says the announcer. "It's time to send the bride and groom off. So, everyone, let's go outside."

Everyone goes outside. The limo driver leaves to get the limo. People line up outside the church. The ushers of the church hand everyone little bags of rice to toss. The wedding party bursts out of the church.

Rice is thrown into the air. Frank waves to his daughter as Hezekiah and Faith hurry to the limo. Cameras flash and everyone smiles, happy for the new couple. The limo with "just married" painted on the back of the window drives away.

Faith gazes at Hezekiah for a second. He moves in close, and his lips lightly touch hers, and they kiss. Their kisses multiply. Hezekiah pulls back.

"Now the real party begins," says Faith. She grabs Hezekiah's belt and slips her fingers in between the fabric.

"Excuse me, but I can see you," says the limo driver.

They both sigh in unison. Faith pulls her hand back to her side. Hezekiah looks for a switch, but there is no privacy panel to raise between the driver and the back seat.

Chapter 24

KEEP THE FAITH

FAITH AND HEZEKIAH RIDE IN THE LIMO TOGETHER. he starts to think about what the ghost said to him. The phrase, "Faith is a dead woman walking," still haunts him. *Is there something in the spirit world that I'm missing? Am I failing Faith right now by being complacent?*

Faith's eyebrows draw together, and she lays her hand on Hezekiah's quad. "What are you thinking about?" asks Faith, softly.

"Nothing, I guess. I just..."

"You 'just' what?"

"I just want you to be safe," says Hezekiah.

"I am safe; I'm riding in a car with you. You are, by far, the strongest man I've ever met. The only other way I would be safer is if I'm in God's presence."

That was a comforting thought for Hezekiah, and at the same time, it was not.

"What's wrong? It's our wedding day. I don't want you to worry. I know what it is; you're thinking about what that demon said again, aren't you?"

"Yes, I am."

"Hezekiah, I don't want you to think about that right now. How many times has someone tried to kill me, human or otherwise? And what happened?"

"I was there to rescue you."

"Exactly. So, can you please stop worrying about it?"

Hezekiah tries, but he still can't shake the thought of her death.

"You know what? Your worrying is starting to worry me. So, I want you to just give me some space right now," she says, frowning.

"But..."

"Give me some space," says Faith, sharply.

Hezekiah backs off and moves to the other side of the limo. They are quiet for the next few minutes as the limo drives through the city. It's a nice clear day outside. As they ride, Hezekiah on one side of the limo, and Faith on the other, they are both wondering how they let the problems of life divide them so fast. As Faith thinks, arms crossed, and staring out the window, Hezekiah prays: *What did I do to cause this separation so fast? Lord God, please help me to fix this. Please show me what I need to do. What did I do to cause this in the first place?*

You don't trust Me to take care of Faith. You must realize that I AM her protector, not you.

Faith turns her head and peers at Hezekiah. "Hezekiah, my life is not in your hands, it's in God's."

Convicted, Hezekiah stays silent. *Lord God, I'm sorry for not trusting You. Why else is Faith mad?*

You're talking about death on your wedding day, God whispers.

Hezekiah clears his throat. "Faith, I'm so sorry. I should not have doubted God, and I should not be talking about you dying on our wedding day. This should be a day of celebration, and instead, I'm turning it into a day of doubt and fear, something that I should not do in the first place. You are right; God is your protector. I shouldn't act as if unless I'm near you, you're dead."

Faith is silent. Frowning, she stares out the window with her arms and legs crossed.

What is she thinking about? Did I say something wrong? What should I do next?

He moves toward her, and the hair on his arms stands on edge. Faith is still quiet, slightly bouncing her leg. Nervous sweat slides down his face as he inches closer to her.

Unmoving, other than her leg, Faith remains quiet, looking out the window. Her jaw is clenched shut.

Hezekiah inches toward her and hesitates. Faith sighs loudly through her nose. The limo finally leaves the city and approaches the house.

"Will you forgive me?"

Faith looks down at the carpet, and her leg stills. She licks her lips and exhales. "Hezekiah, it's tough to stay mad at you. But please don't do that again. You've been talking about me dying and getting me worried about my own life. You've been doing it for a while, and it's been in the back of my mind all day. So please don't do it again." She turns toward him. A tear runs down her face.

Hezekiah rushes toward Faith and slowly puts his arm around her shoulders. "I'm sorry. I should not have been doing that, and I didn't mean to worry you. I was selfish to think that something like that wouldn't be bothering you. I am sorry for being so careless. I won't do it again."

"Just remember to have faith in God. You're the Spirit Warrior," she says, readjusting Hezekiah's shirt collar. "It's not a good look for you to start doubting the God you fight for. Also, you not trusting God is unattractive to me."

"Oh," he says, opening his eyes a little wider.

"You are so confident when you follow God that it makes people want to follow you. It makes me want to follow you. So, don't lose your faith, okay?"

Hezekiah ponders Faith's words.

Faith smiles. "It also makes you look sexy."

"What?" He smiles and blushes.

"Yeah. When I see you practicing with your sword, it drives me wild. I get excited when I see you working out without your shirt."

The limo pulls up to the house, and the driver parks. He gets out and opens the door for them. Faith and Hezekiah step out into the warm air. He thanks the driver for his services, and the driver gets back into the limo. They both wave at the departing limo. Hezekiah sweeps Faith off her feet and cradles her.

"Our humble abode awaits," says Faith.

Chapter 25

THE WAIT IS OVER

HEZEKIAH CARRIES FAITH OVER THE THRESHOLD of the front door of the house. She jumps out of his arms and runs into the living room. Her eyes sparkle. She looks at the amount of work done to the house's interior.

"Is this really the same house? It's so clean!"

The walls have been scrubbed and repainted white. The brown hardwood floors have been cleaned and polished. Portraits of flowers decorate the walls throughout the house.

"Hezekiah, how did you get all this done so fast?"

"When you have a cleaning crew working around the clock, it's quite easy," he says.

Faith prances around the downstairs and returns to the living room. On the fireplace mantel, she finds a bouquet of roses. Faith smells the fresh, crisp scent of the roses. Next to them, she sees a few empty picture frames.

"Why are all these picture frames empty?"

Hezekiah steps in front of her, gazes into her eyes, and softly holds her face. Faith's skin tingles. "These are for the beautiful memories that will be." Hezekiah holds the small of her back and gently presses her body into his. Faith arches her back. He leans in and kisses her lips softly, using his lips to softly brush hers. He locks lips with her, and their kisses deepen. She starts to sweat. He removes his jacket. His lips touch and sample the neck, and she exhales. Fluttery sensations envelop her chest and stomach. Faith's heart pounds into her chest. She reaches with her fingers in between the buttons of his shirt, touches his flesh, pops his shirt loose, and removes his shirt. Hezekiah unzips the back of her dress. Faith fumbles with his belt, loosens it, and unbuttons his pants. Hezekiah slowly pulls back and exhales.

"I haven't shown you the best part of the house." Hezekiah scoops her off her feet and carries her upstairs. The bedroom walls are painted a lush red. The furniture and sheets on the mattress are white. On the floor, a path of rose petals leads to a bed covered in them. The rich wine scent of the rose petals permeates the room. Hezekiah lays her on the bed and lays next to her. Hezekiah kisses her and caresses her arms. Faith shivers. Hezekiah slides off part of her dress. They grow hot and feverish. Hezekiah and Faith kiss and caress, exploring each other.

Chapter 26

UNKNOWN SICKNESS

AT THE CHURCH, PEOPLE ARE IN THE PROCESS OF leaving, and a limo arrives. The governor rubs his chest and exits his limo. People leave the church as he walks toward the stairs. People's laughter echoes through the air. The governor remembers Catherine and breaking the news to her family. Her parents and her only child wailed. As he remembers this, a few of his staff from the departing crowd head toward him.

"Governor, sir, are you okay?" asks Alex, his chief of staff.

"No." Roxbury bows his head. His grief aches throughout his body.

"What's wrong?"

Frank and Ms. Hyatt walk outside.

"Governor Roxbury, how—" Alex holds up his hand. He and Ms. Hyatt both stare at the governor.

Alex walks closer, but the governor holds his hand up. "Sir, what's wrong?"

Roxbury lifts his head. His crystal blue eyes flood. "Catherine is dead."

Alex gasps.

"How did this happen?" asks Alex.

"She was sick with a virus that went around the office. She seemed fine at first, but now she's gone." The governor struggles to hold his own thoughts together amidst stabbing head pressure.

"I don't mean to sound insensitive here, but weren't there other people close to Catherine before she got sick?" asks Alex.

"Yes, a lot of... a lot of people in the office. Which is why I'm... I'm here now," says the governor.

Frank scans the governors face. Roxbury's usual stately and robust appearance has been replaced by a hunched-over old man. "Are you okay, Governor?"

"I'm fine. We need to warn the pub... the pub... public..." The governor collapses into Alex's arms.

"Call an ambulance, hurry!" shouts Alex.

Chapter 27

MEDICAL EMERGENCY

FRANK INSTINCTIVELY MOVES EVERYONE OUT OF the way and assesses the situation as Ms. Hyatt calls an ambulance. The governor's security detail makes a protective circle around the scene. Minutes later, the ambulance arrives. Paramedics load Roxbury onto a stretcher and attach emergency equipment to the governor. Alex jumps into the ambulance, and the vehicle speeds off.

———————◆———————

Minutes later, the paramedics burst into the ER. They weave through the crowd. The governor's breathing shallows. His heart stops, and then he stops breathing. They burst into the room and insist that Alex stays outside. Paramedics perform chest compressions. They quickly get the defibrillators and attach the pads to his body. His cardiac monitor flatlines. Defibrillators charge and shock his body. No response. A nurse performs chest compressions and rescue breaths. The AED announces a shock. The pads charge and deliver a shock. No cardiac response. The nurse continues with chest compressions and rescue breaths. The governor's skin turns blue.

Alex listens from the hallway. "Darn it! Do something to save his life!" shouts Alex.

"We are doing the best we can. Give us some time," says the paramedic.

Chest compressions continue. AED charges for another shock. A technician motions for everyone to stand back.

"Clear!"

Electricity jolts through Roxbury's body.

All stare at the cardiac monitor for signs of life.

"Well?!" shouts Alex.

The monitor beeps once, twice, and three times; the governor's cardiac signs steady as his breathing returns.

"Oh, thank God," says Alex.

"He's not out of the woods yet. We still need to find out what is causing this sickness, and he is still struggling to breathe."

Roxbury's heartbeat goes erratic, sending paramedics into a panic. The governor seizes and flops violently. The nurses secure his head. Roxbury's body flounders.

"Jesus, please save the governor's life!" shouts Alex.

The governor stops shaking. He inhales hard and opens his eyes, then exhales and slumps on the bed. The doctors step back and observe his condition. The governor closes his eyes, and his vital signs normalize. The doctors scratch their heads.

"Thank you, God," says Alex.

Chapter 28

HOSPITAL STAY

THE NEXT DAY, WHILE THE GOVERNOR IS IN ICU, His health slowly creeps back; grieving over Catherine, a tear runs down his cheek. He has the thought to contact his press secretary. As he reaches for his cell phone, a doctor urges him to rest.

"Ma'am, I can't rest; I have to let my staff know what's going on."

"We've already done that, sir. Just relax."

"People must know about this sickness."

"Sir," the doctor says, "we don't know if what you have is contagious or not. We've ruled out a few diseases, but we don't know what you have yet."

"Doc, all I know is that half of my staff is out sick because of this bug going around. And the other half may be next. Also, there have been a lot of people in and out of the capitol. I need to let the staff know to shut everything down."

"Sir, all of your staff is in this hospital," says the doctor.

"What?"

"They have been here 'round the clock to not only check on you but also to check on each other. We've been hospitalizing people here at an alarming rate. Some people were able to leave, but some people are still extremely sick."

"Where have I been?"

"You've been asleep. We didn't know whether or not you would make it at first."

"Okay. Doctor, do me this favor. Call *Central City News* and have them send me a reporter as soon as possible. We need to let people know that we have an outbreak of epic proportions. We need to initiate a lockdown immediately until we can find out what this is and its cause."

"Sir, your chief of staff is here. He is already in the process of setting one up."

Chapter 29

LOVE'S COCOON & OUTSIDE WORRIES

FAITH AND HEZEKIAH AWAKEN TOGETHER IN their bed. The sun cascades into the room from the balcony. Hezekiah softly combs his fingers through her hair and across her arms. Warmth spreads through her body. Faith gently rests her hands on his chest. They both lay there enjoying the morning sun. He holds her close.

"Good morning," says Hezekiah softly. He gazes into her brown eyes and gently brushes a strand of hair from her face.

"Good morning to you," says Faith, smiling. She peers into his brown eyes, getting lost into them.

The atmosphere is electric between them. She is glad Hezekiah took his time. Faith held out on sex for a long time, even with men who had great wealth and status. Now, staring at the man of her dreams, she is glad she waited.

"So, what do you want to do today?" asks Hezekiah above a whisper.

"I don't know. What do you have in mind?" asks Faith, smiling.

"I thought we could go hiking in the mountains. Just the two of us."

"That sounds nice. Maybe we should go this morning," says Faith.

"Okay. I guess we should get ready to go." Hezekiah lifts his head and gives Faith a soft peck on the lips, which sends warm flutters through her body. She kisses him back, and warm tingles travel from his lips and cascades down his neck. Faith exhales.

"Okay, if we continue this, we won't make it out of bed," says Faith.

"You're right, let's go."

Twenty minutes later, after a shower, they leave the bed room in hiking gear and stroll to the front door. They both reach for the door-knob simultaneously, and their hands touch. A pleasant shock jolts through them both. The air between them electrifies. Hezekiah puts his hand on her arm and causes tingles to vibrate through her body. Faith exhales. He tilts his head and kisses Faith, and she loses herself in his arms. Hezekiah's hands travel, and Faith gasps. Their kisses multiply, and they forget all about the mountains.

Frank's at home alone. He thinks about Ms. Hyatt for a moment and their upcoming date. His mind shifts to the governor. His grief after the death of Catherine has destroyed him. Frank decides to check on the governor. He searches for his keys. A few minutes later, after finding his keys, he decides to turn on the TV. Alex is conducting a press conference.

Alex, outside the hospital, is preparing to address the news. Not knowing what may come from his announcement, he tries to choose his words carefully.

"We are always here as public servants to serve the people of this region. That may not always be easy at times, considering that we were in the midst of an invasion not too long ago. With that being said, it's with a heavy heart I announce that this city is in yet another crisis."

The press core gasp and murmur.

"Please settle down," says Alex.

"What kind of crisis is it? Are we being invaded again?" asks a reporter from *Central City News*.

"No. This time, the problem is from within. We don't quite know the origin, but a virus has broken out. Right now, we are doing everything in our power to contain this threat, but it's spreading rapidly. We..."

"So, what is your plan? What does the governor plan to do?"

"Let me get to that. We are in the process of finding a solution for our situation , but in the meantime, we need everyone to stay calm. If you are sick, stay home and call 911. Emergency crews will come to you. Don't go out if you don't need to. Today, because the problem extends beyond the walls of this hospital, there will be a 10:00 pm curfew."

"What else do you plan to do?"

"That's it for now. We will let you know of more when the time comes."

Alex ends the press conference. Reporters rumble with questions, but Alex walks away.

Frank turns off the television. "Oh my God."

Chapter 30

ROAD TRIP

IN THE AFTERNOON, FAITH AND HEZEKIAH WALK out the front door and take supplies to the Jeep. Instead of a trip to the mountains, they make plans to travel to the beach. They pack food, extra clothes, and hygiene products. They close the door of the Jeep and head toward the coast. Faith is wearing a light blue one-piece bathing suit and tan shorts. Hezekiah is wearing a white tank top, blue swimming shorts, and black sandals. Faith glances over to his muscular body and exhales. Faith pitches herself to focus as she drives. Leaving town, Hezekiah spots a shimmering figure from the corner of his eye and turns his head. Faith glances at Hezekiah staring out the window, muscles tensing.

"Baby," says Faith softly. "What's wrong? You look like you've seen a ghost."

Hezekiah turns his head. "Oh, no, sweetie, I'm fine. I just want us to focus on our honeymoon."

Something tells Faith to inquire. "Hezekiah, I know we are on our honeymoon, but I also realize that you are the Spirit Warrior. I know I was upset before, but now I'm ready to hear what you have to say."

"It's probably nothing, but I thought I saw something strange."

"What?"

"For a split second, I thought I saw two angels carrying someone into the air."

Faith squints. She turns her eyes back to the road. "Is that so?"

"Yeah. Maybe I just fell asleep for a second."

"No, I believe you. Remember who you are talking to. Jesus appeared in my father's backyard not that long ago. So, I believe you." *I wonder what's going to come from this?*

"Well, let's not worry about that now; let's just focus on going to the beach," says Hezekiah.

As the two continue down the road, he looks at Faith and puts his hand on her thigh. She smiles and keeps driving. Hezekiah sees a road sign that leads to the City of Light. Faith takes a turn to head that way. Two hours later, after much light-hearted small talk, they arrive at a beach town right off the desert.

"Thanks for driving here. It means a lot to me," says Hezekiah. "This place brings back memories."

"You said we should go to the beach for our honeymoon, didn't you?" says Faith. Hezekiah smiles. They pass by the road sign "The City of Light."

Chapter 31

THE COAST

AT THE COAST, FAITH PARKS THE JEEP. HEZEKIAH gets out and opens the door for her. He gets the towels and food basket from the back seat, and they walk to the beach. The soft, hot sand sifts across their feet. They walk midway toward the water and set up their beach camp. Hezekiah puts down a towel for Faith to sit on. He puts down the basket, gives Faith a bottle of water, and sits himself. They gaze out to the coast. Hezekiah inches his arm around the small of her back, and they relax. He studies her and smiles. Faith turns to him.

"What?" she asks.

"I'm just wondering how you thought of coming to this beach in particular."

"Well, it is the one you recommended at the wedding; it's the closest beach to where we live, and besides, I like this beach. My parents used to bring me here when I was a kid. That was before the town went crazy."

"What happened?"

"My parents brought me here, and Dad was talking to us about Jesus when some angry sheriff came over. He threatened to arrest my dad for saying 'Jesus.' My dad ignored him. The sheriff got upset and pulled out a pair of handcuffs to try to arrest my dad."

"What?"

"My dad started herding us to the car. While we were moving to the car, the sheriff grabbed him and tried to put handcuffs on my dad."

"What do you mean tried?"

My dad shoved him to the ground and ran to the car with us. However, things took a turn for the worse."

"What happened?"

"The sheriff pointed a gun at us!"

"What?"

"Yeah. However, when he pulled the trigger, nothing happened. I saw the sheriff check his gun. My father sped off. That was the last time my parents and I came to this beach. That was the last time I came to the coast with my mother." Faith's mouth dries and she starts to cough. Hezekiah draws her close to his chest. She rests in his arms, and they stare into the sunset.

"I'm okay, thank you," says Faith.

A cop gazes at them and begins to stroll over from a distance.

Hezekiah rubs her back, which sends tingles down her spine. He then kisses her forehead. They watch the ocean waves break on the shore.

"You know, it's stunning out here. Did you ever come out here while you were in the city?" asks Faith.

"Once," he says.

"Really, why only once?"

Hezekiah gazes off into the sunset. "When I arrived in this city, the drama I encountered was nonstop from start to finish. I had to encounter demons of all kinds; I went to jail, escaped an underground graveyard, and faced Moloch before I could sit down and think."

"It sounds like you really had a wild ride in this town," says Faith.

"Yes, he did," says a man standing above them. They both stare at the dark silhouette. He has olive-toned skin and red hair.

Energy spikes through Hezekiah's body. He jumps up to his feet. Faith jumps to her feet. The cop unsheathes a large sword, and Hezekiah summons the Sword of the Spirit.

"I knew it was you," says the cop. He smiles and puts his sword away. He holds out his hands.

"Hezekiah, do you know this guy?" asks Faith.

Hezekiah glares at him, and his face brightens. "Oh, it's you!"

Chapter 32

THE CITY OF LIGHT

"LONG TIME NO SEE, HEZEKIAH! HOW HAVE YOU been?" asks the cop.

Faith wonders who this man is. Hezekiah and the cop exchange hugs. He has dark blue armor, and he carries a glowing sky blue sword. She thinks back to a call she made to the City of Light a while ago. She starts to put two and two together about this officer.

"Are you Jason?" asks Faith.

"Faith, I'm sorry, this is Jason, the Spirit Warrior of the City of Light. And Jason, this is my beautiful wife, Faith," says Hezekiah.

"It's nice to meet you," she says.

"The pleasure is mine," says Jason. "I heard a rumor that you got married. I didn't know it was true. I heard about you calling here about a court trial you were going through not too long ago, but we were dealing with a crisis at the time."

"What happened?" asks Hezekiah.

"Death," Jason's smile flees his face.

"What does that mean?" asks Faith.

"The spirit of Death came strong on this city."

"What? How? I thought everyone in this city got saved," says Hezekiah.

"Yes, however, that doesn't mean we were immune from dying. That version of Death you fought over six months ago pales in comparison to the version of Death I just got through fighting," says Jason.

"Really?"

"Wait, wait, wait," says Faith. "You had to fight the spirit of Death?"

"Yes, I did. It was a hard battle too. I wasn't his target, though. Jesus put me in jail so that I could witness to some people," says Hezekiah.

"Is that how that happened?" asks Jason. "That entire night was filled with chaos."

"How so?" asks Faith.

"Death shot down from the sky and burst into the prison cafeteria. He killed everyone in there and went throughout the prison, killing different people."

"I didn't know all that happened," says Hezekiah.

"Oh my, yes. That night, everyone was on edge. People were either trying to leave, hide, or get more ammunition. It was a scary night. When you escaped, it added pressure to the situation. In fact, after Greg died, we thought you were connected to his death."

"I was," says Hezekiah, frowning.

"What do you mean?" asked Jason.

"Well, he was one of the people I was sent to witness to about Jesus."

"What happened?" asks Faith.

"I slipped into the tower he was working in. I witnessed to him about Jesus, and he knocked me out the window. I fell into the greenhouse below. I then heard the tower explode."

"Oh, Hezekiah, it's not your fault that he died. It was just his time," says Faith.

"That's just it. He could have lived longer if he had just accepted God's salvation. If I had said something different, maybe he could have..."

"Don't blame yourself for his choice," says Faith. She rubs Hezekiah's back. "Remember, God gives us the words to say when we get into situations like that. His heart was closed to God already. You were just a way to confirm what God had already known."

Jason smiles, witnessing the couple in action.

"What happened with you and Death?" asks Hezekiah.

"Let me start from the beginning. After you left the city, everyone received salvation. It was like living in heaven on earth for a little while. However, God was calling people to move away so they could be salt and light in other places. About half of the saved people moved out and went to other places. We prayed for them and wished them well. However, the people who moved in were evil. They started doing awful things in the city and even led some of our Christian brothers and sisters astray. Anyway, in the process of time, the spirit of Death and his minions came up against us so strong that a lot of people died," says Jason.

"What did Death's minions look like?"

"They looked like angels dressed in white robes, but they had teeth like lions," says Jason.

Hezekiah thinks about his fight with the ghost. *Could the spirit of Death be after Faith?*

Faith puts a hand on his shoulder.

"How did you defeat Death?" asks Hezekiah.

Jason shifts his head back.

"How did you defeat Death?" asks Faith.

"I didn't."

"What?" asks Hezekiah.

"Why do you sound so surprised? Fighting Death is not like fighting another evil spirit. He is very tricky. At first, people started dying off with sickness everywhere. Then random people started dying from a stroke, heart attack, or just being struck down by something. I was too overwhelmed to handle the situation until God told me what to do. I asked God why so many people were dying. In so many words, God told me that Satan had asked to sift the city like wheat."

"What did you do?" asks Hezekiah.

"I had to go door to door, witnessing to people about the salvation of Jesus. At the same time, Death was striking people down in different parts of the city. As people received Christ, the spirit of Death would leave them. That's how I got the leg armor you see me in now. In fact, I was witnessing to a woman..." Jason turns his head away, and his throat constricts. Hezekiah puts his hand on his shoulder. "I was witnessing to a woman when Death physically burst into her home." Jason clears his throat. His eyes swell. "Death burst into her home. I'll never forget the ghastly sight. He had the face of a skeleton and was dressed in a shadowy, black cloak. He charged at her with a sickle. I countered, and we fought like crazy. He was swift, faster than I had anticipated. Even with me moving as fast as lightning, it was hard to counter his attacks. We burst out of the house and fought on the roof of the house. We clashed weapons, he glared into my eyes, and that's when..." He gets quiet, shakes his head, and puts his hand on his head. "That's when it happened."

"What?" asks Faith.

"Like I said before, what Hezekiah fought in prison, not too long ago, was only a taste of what we had to go through in this city. Death showed me a vision of the lady's death and how she would die."

Faith and Hezekiah glance at each other and back at Jason.

"I rushed back to the lady, and..." His throat dries up but forces himself to continue. "I found her in a pool of her own blood."

Faith puts a hand over her mouth. Jason coughs and puts a hand over his. He turns his back.

Hezekiah puts his hand on his shoulder. "You did the best you could."

"Did I?" says Jason, eyes wide. "I was so wrapped up in the battle that I forgot to protect the young lady."

"You can't do it all, Jason. Don't blame yourself. You did what God wanted you to do. You're not God. And even if you were, the choice to accept Christ was hers to make."

"But she made that choice for Jesus. Why did she still die?" asks Jason.

"I don't know, but she's in God's hands. And that's the safest place she can be," says Faith.

Jason glances toward heaven. His eyes clear, and his voice returns. "How did we get on such a depressing topic? I should be happy you are here."

A boy walks up. "Hezekiah! Is that really you?"

The three of them look over, and Immanuel comes and hugs Hezekiah.

"How are you? I thought I would never see you again," says Immanuel.

"Same here," says Hezekiah.

The four of them talk about old times. Immanuel brings up how Hezekiah received the sword of the Spirit. Jason talks about how he chased Hezekiah into the cave of Moloch. They laugh and joke about how Jason and Hezekiah were at odds in the cave. The conversation turns to how Hezekiah saved Immanuel from Moloch and how Jesus appeared to fight against the demon. They talk on and on until the sun goes down. Jason takes the new couple out to dinner and reacquaint further.

Since it's late, Hezekiah decides to get a hotel off the beach. Faith and Hezekiah enter the room and take off their shoes. The blue carpet rubs their feet. The blue and white sheets of the king-sized bed match the carpet. The room has a balcony facing the ocean.

"They really do nail the theme of the ocean in this room," says Hezekiah.

Faith chuckles a little and smiles at him.

"What? I was serious," he says, laughing a little.

"Okay. I'm going to freshen up," says Faith. She kisses Hezekiah. The kiss warms his face. Faith grabs and pulls back the liner of his shorts and lets go. The elastic pops his stomach. She walks into the bathroom and turns on the shower. Hezekiah follows her into the bathroom and joins her.

Chapter 33

DOWNTOWN

THE NEXT MORNING, FAITH AND HEZEKIAH awaken after a long night of passion, wrapped in each other's arms.

"Good morning, beautiful," says Hezekiah as he cups her face in his hands.

"Good morning, baby," says Faith as she gently caresses his face.

For a brief moment, he remembers what Jason said about the spirit of Death, and his mouth dries and causes him to frown.

"What's wrong?" asks Faith, squinting her eyes.

The thought of Faith dying turns his stomach. He determines within himself to protect her, no matter what the cost. Unwilling to worry her, he tunes out the negative thoughts and changes the subject.

"I'm okay, beautiful."

"Okay," says Faith. She kisses him.

"There is somewhere I want to visit today," says Hezekiah.

"Where?"

"I want to visit the city council building."

"Why?"

"I have friends in the city council I want to see. They're so busy that if we don't go to them, I won't be able to see them."

"Okay," says Faith, shrugging her shoulders.

"Besides, It's in a beautiful area at the base of the mountain."

"Okay, an outdoors sightseeing tour. That sounds good," says Faith. Her face brightens at the thought of a nature walk.

"Good. You won't be disappointed."

The couple get up, shower, and get dressed. They check out of the hotel and drive toward the city council building.

"This city has really changed," says Hezekiah.

"In what way?"

"This place used to be a town with a lot of dirt roads. Now it's a bustling metropolis."

"Okay, that may be a bit of a stretch. I see some tall buildings, but this is not a big city."

"It's not a huge city, no. However, I'm not used to driving around town here. Everyone walked everywhere. There were no cars."

Faith puts her hand on Hezekiah's leg. "Baby, I think you're used to not driving here because you had no one to drive you."

"No, I'm serious. A lot of people walked here."

"Well, this is a beach town, after all."

Faith continues to drive, and Hezekiah directs her. Road construction blocks their way to the city council building. They find a parking deck a few blocks away. Faith drives inside and parks her Jeep. They exit the vehicle, and a few minutes later, exit the parking deck. They stand at the sidewalk to cross the street. The "Don't Walk" sign on the pedestrian traffic light is on. They wait, and Hezekiah has another thought about Faith's death. He tries to block it out, but now it's blaring. Hezekiah frowns.

"Hezekiah, what's wrong?"

"I'm... okay."

Faith frowns. *Is he thinking about what Jason said yesterday?* She gently places her palm on his face. She peers into his eyes. "Hezekiah, I love you, and I know that you love me. However, I don't want you to worry about me. We have been through danger, time and time again, and I'm not dead yet. I cannot die unless God says so. So, please stop worrying for me."

Hezekiah smiles, but then frowns. Thoughts of her death shoot through his mind. Faith sucks her teeth and exhales. She throws her hands in the air and walks across the street.

"Faith, look out!"

A speeding car zooms at Faith! Faith screams. The driver slams on the brakes. She closes her eyes. Faith is struck! Her body caroms sideways. Feeling numb, her body ascends into the air.

Oh my God, I'm dead, I'm dead!

Chapter 34

HIDDEN ENEMY

FAITH PLUMMETS FAST AND TUMBLES THROUGH the air. Arms flailing, she panics. *I'm I going to hell?* She jolts to a stop. Heavy breathing echoes into her ear. Applause bursts through Faith's ears, and she opens her eyes. She's in Hezekiah's arms.

"Faith, are you okay?" he asks, with a frown.

"Yeah I..." she looks at Hezekiah, noticing that he's biting his lip. She hugs his neck.

"Oh my God, oh my God, oh my God."

"Faith, it's okay calm down? Are you hurt?"

"No, I'm not hurt." Hezekiah stands, holding her in his arms. Tears stream down her face.

"Is she going to be okay?" asks a pedestrian.

"We're fine; we just need some space," says Hezekiah.

A police officer comes over and disperses the crowd.

More people gather and check on them. From the distance, a figure hovering in the air observes the happy scene. He sneers.

"Hezekiah, you always ruin everything!" says the evil spirit, Murder. He flies off into the air as he plots, waiting for another opportune time to kill Faith. "I know exactly what I'll do next."

Chapter 35

PAST PLOT

THE CROWD GIVES THEM THEIR SPACE, AND THEY leave. Faith calms herself and stands.

"Hey are you okay? We can go back home if you..."

"No... no. I don't feel like driving right now, and you wanted to see your council friends. It'll help me take my mind off of what just happened."

"Okay."

Hezekiah and Faith make their way to the council building. A few minutes later, they arrive.

"This place looks like a palace," says Faith. The limestone council building sits at the base of the mountain. It shines in the sunlight like a jewel. The polished stone steps lead to the red double doors of the council building. They walk up the stairs. The double doors open, and three of the council members walk out. They take a second glance at Hezekiah and Faith. Their eyes widen.

"Hey! Hezekiah is out here!" shouts Ahithophel, the oldest council member. His silver hair shines in the sun. A few more people run outside and usher Hezekiah and Faith into the building. Hezekiah gets reacquainted with them. They exchange greetings as they laugh together.

Faith glances at their faces and can't help study the sparkle in their eyes and smile on their faces. *This city must have been through a lot.*

They invite Faith and Hezekiah for drinks on the outside patio. As Hezekiah talks to his friends, Faith's mind shifts to Jason and his prior conversation with Hezekiah. Thoughts of him battling Death flash through her mind. Also, images of the speeding car flash through her head. She closes her eyes and rubs her face, but the thoughts race through her head quickly. The car speeds toward her to hit her!

"Excuse me, young lady? Are you okay?" asks Ahithophel.

"Yeah... I'm... I'm fine."

"You look like you have a headache. Are you sure everything is okay?"

"Yes... no."

"What's wrong?"

"I want to know something."

"What is it?" asks Ahithophel.

"From your perspective, why did the spirit of Death attack this city? What was happening here that caused something so terrible to happen?"

"Well, that, young lady, is an excellent question. First, you must understand that just because someone is a Christian doesn't mean they are immune to dying. Remember, Jesus died but was resurrected. However, with that being said, a lot of the people who moved here were either atheists or practiced witchcraft."

"Really?" asks Faith. "From what Hezekiah said before about what he saved this city from, how come you didn't just outlaw such practices?"

"As a free city, we don't impose laws against what people choose to do. Also, you can't outlaw someone's thoughts. If someone chooses to be an atheist, you cannot force them to believe in God. It's impossible.

However, the consequences of their choices were arrayed in full display when death started to rain down on our city-state, on Christians and non-Christians alike."

"How so? How come everyone died together?"

"I don't know, young lady. I suppose it was a combination of things. Some people were old, while other people started to compromise with unbelievers by doing things they were not supposed to do. In the end, a lot of people ended up dying."

"I don't feel like I'm getting a clear answer. I know that God will judge a city, but what happened in the natural that caused people to die?" asks Faith.

"We found out there was a witch who cast spells on people and showed himself as great. Many people flocked to him, and started casting their own spells to create wealth and success in their lives. We also found out through numerous sources that they used human blood to do these spells. As the witchcraft started to increase, the entire town council spoke out against it," says Ahithophel.

"Okay, so how come it didn't stop?"

"We were all voted out of office. It was only after all this drama came to a close that we were reinstated. But I digress. The same witch who started the problem became the city leader, and we were persecuted. Eventually, we were pressured into silence. As witchcraft continued to abound, people started to die, but not in mass numbers. One day, as I remember, Jason fought his way into City Hall at the height of the witchcraft and challenged the witch. The fight spilled out into the street, and Jason won. However, it was too little too late," says Ahithophel.

"What do you mean?"

"You would think that defeating the head conspirator would loosen Satan's grip on the town. However, because so many people willingly chose to become witches themselves, they turned on Jason and tried to kill him. They not only turned on him, but they also turned on every single Christian in town. They started to kill us."

"Okay, why does your version of this story sound different than Jason's?"

"What, young lady, are you referring to?"

"Jason said nothing about what you just described. What you described is a full-on necromantic seduction of half the people in the city. Also, he said that the spirit of Death physically manifested and started killing people."

"You didn't let me finish. As the witches were hunting us, one of them thought it was a marvelous idea for them to summon the spirit of Death to kill us."

Faith gasps. She puts her hand over her mouth. "How are people able to control the spirit of Death? Isn't he like a fallen angel or something?"

"That, my dear, is an easy question to answer. They can't. I'm deducing that it was Satan's plan all along. When they summoned Death, a dreadful thing happened to them."

"What?"

"They were all massacred. Death quickly killed all the witches. Death and his cohorts floated about and planned to kill the rest of us in the city. That's where Jason stepped in. Through the power of God, he was able to save a lot of people in the city and defeat the spirit of Death."

"Wait, Jason said that he didn't defeat Death."

"Why would he possibly say that?"

"He started talking about a woman he was witnessing to who died."

"Oh." Ahithophel exhales. "That young lady Jason referred to was the love of his life."

Faith glances at Hezekiah. He's talking and laughing with the other members of the council.

"How do you know?" asks Faith.

"He used to talk about her a lot. She was well known in the community for speaking up for Christians but wasn't one herself. Jason took notice of her, and they became romantic. He would have us pray for her that she would get saved. However, I don't think she ever accepted

Christ. From what I can tell, he was not successful in rescuing her from death, which is why he feels like he failed."

"That's a real sad story."

"Indeed. I wonder how Hezekiah would feel if he lost you," says Ahithophel.

Faith gasps. Unable to respond, she starts to understand why Hezekiah is a little overprotective. Seeing Jason in such a sad state gives her a new insight into how Hezekiah feels.

As the bright sun reaches noon zenith in the sky, the couple says their goodbyes to the city council and head home.

Chapter 36

NEW PLOT

FAITH AND HEZEKIAH ARRIVE AT FRANK'S HOUSE. They think about the day and the conversations they had with Hezekiah's old friends. Faith thinks about her conversation with Ahithophel. The thought of an attack by the spirit of Death causes her to frown. Hezekiah gets out of the Jeep and opens the door for her. She climbs out and smiles at him. They go inside the house. Frank greets them, smiling, and offers them lemonade. They all sit down together in the living room.

"So, how was your honeymoon?" asks Frank.

"It was great," they say in unison.

Please don't ask where we went after the wedding, thinks Faith.

"Where did you go after the wedding?" asks Frank.

Faith clears her throat and coughs. Hezekiah scratches the back of his neck and turns his head. They both try to speak, but they interrupt each other. Frank covers his mouth to hide a chuckle. Faith exhales.

Faith squares her shoulders. "We went to the beach in the City of Light," Faith says.

"Yeah, we ran into old friends," says Hezekiah.

"I got the chance to meet all of Hezekiah's old friends and work associates. It was quite interesting." She smirks.

"Well, I'm glad you had fun. So, what did you do after the beach?"

"We went to dinner with them," says Faith.

"What did you do after that?" he asks with a smile.

Faith's gaze narrows, and a vein appears on the side of her head. Frank laughs.

"Well, I'm glad you enjoyed your vacation away from the city. Both of you needed it. After the last conflict you had with Warlord, you were due one," says Frank, smiling. His smile drops into a frown.

"Dad, is there something you're not telling us?" asks Faith.

"I didn't want to burden you so quickly, but since you left, the city is on the verge of a new crisis."

"What do you mean?" asks Hezekiah, sharpening his eyes.

"An unknown virus is quickly spreading throughout the city. No one knows where it came from or what's causing it. All we know is that it is highly contagious and deadly," says Frank.

This must be what God was warning me about not too long ago, Hezekiah thinks.

"I can't help to think that this has a spiritual component to it," says Frank.

"You're right, but in what way are you thinking?" asks Faith.

"Think about it, you two. After Warlord was defeated, was there a huge spiritual revival after he was destroyed?"

"Not that I know of. In fact, the city kind of went back to business as usual. Other than Hezekiah being a new celebrity for saving the city, people are not really that into God any more than before," says

Faith. "Don't get me wrong. God did get a lot of people's attention, but a lot more people are still on the fence, which is why they could still be vulnerable."

"That's true," says Hezekiah.

"Hezekiah, what is the difference between you saving the City of Light and Central City?" asks Frank.

"Quite a few differences, actually. When that city was saved, they knew that it was Jesus and not me who saved them from destruction."

"How so?"

"When I first got there, I was given the sword of the Spirit and had to fight a tiger-shaped demon in the middle of the street. Shortly after, I was arrested for preaching in the name of Jesus."

"So, they knew you were a Christian."

"Yes. What added to this was the battle between Moloch and me. At one point during the battle, Jesus showed Himself through me, fought against Moloch, and killed him," says Hezekiah.

"What do you mean? You mean He showed Himself strong by using you to defeat Moloch?"

"No. What I mean is that He enveloped me in an image of Himself as He fought Moloch. Immanuel told me I was hit by an explosive bolt of lightning, and I disappeared. When the lightning faded, everyone saw Jesus instead of me."

"Oh," says Frank.

"So, when the final battle in that city came and went, everyone knew Jesus was responsible for their salvation. In this city, however, they didn't get a chance to see that. People know I represent Jesus and saved the city. But some don't necessarily believe that Jesus is the one responsible for their lives being spared. I'll say one more thing on this; the final battle with Warlord, as far as I know, was not broadcasted on TV. The only way people know that I succeeded after they emerged from the underground is because they are still alive. In the final battle in the City of Light, people could see because they were outside when the evil army was obliterated."

"So, what do you think we should do?" asks Faith.

"We need to have a revival," says Frank. "We need to point people to Jesus so they can be saved."

"Yeah, but saved people still get sick and die. So how would that stop a viral outbreak?" asks Faith.

A scripture pops into Hezekiah's head. "The Bible says in 2 Chronicles 7:13: 'When I shut up the heavens so that there is no rain, or command locusts to devour the land or send a plague among my people, if my people, who are called by my name, will humble themselves and pray and seek my face and turn from their wicked ways, then I will hear from heaven, and I will forgive their sin and will heal their land.' So, we do need to have a revival. Medicine can only do so much for a virus before it mutates. We need God's hand to save us from this situation. And thanks to God, I know how to get this started," says Hezekiah.

"Ah, that's right, you work for Central City Church!" says Faith.

"Yeah! You can get with the pastor tomorrow and set this up—"

A loud buzz interrupts Frank. He looks at his phone and sighs.

"What is it?" asks Faith.

"I have to make rounds at the hospital. They've had a large influx of sick people and can't handle the overflow. So, they're calling me in. Since it's late, please stay here for tonight and make yourselves at home." Frank gets up. "I'll probably see you in the morning." He says goodbye to them and leaves. Moments later, he returns. "Have you seen my car keys?"

Faith gets up, helps him look, and finds the keys in the chair. She takes the spare key off the chain.

"Thanks, dear," says Frank.

"Dad, I'm going to leave a spare car key here on the coffee table just in case."

"Thanks, dear," says Frank, and he leaves the house.

They sit there thinking about what might lie ahead. Faith glances at Hezekiah. He seems to be lost in thought and has a sour glare on his face. She whispers in his ear, his eyes open wide, and he chuckles.

"Why are you whispering? It's not like anyone can hear you," says Hezekiah, smiling.

Faith pats him on the leg and smiles. "Well, I'm going to bed. Follow me if you dare?" She runs into the bedroom, and Hezekiah chases her.

Outside of the house, the evil spirit, Murder, frowns.

"What the—" shouts the demon. Filthy language pours out of his mouth like water. He puts his hands over his face, shuts his eyes, and slides his hand through his white hair.

Chain, another evil spirit, joins him. "What gives?" Chain asks.

"They're spending the night!" shouts Murder.

"So?"

"I had a drunk driver set up to crash into Faith and kill her on impact."

He chuckles. "So much for that. It looks like you're going to have to do something else. Too bad, though. If it weren't for Hezekiah, she would be dead by now. Too bad you can't get rid of him."

Murder stares at him and smiles.

"Oh no. I see that look in your eyes. You know what happened to the last guy who faced Hezekiah head-on."

"I don't care. If I am going to kill Faith, I have to get rid of Hezekiah. In fact, I got an idea, but I need your help to do it."

Chapter 37

A REVIVAL, MAYBE?

AFTER A LONG AND PASSION-FILLED NIGHT, Hezekiah awakens a little tired. Sun streaks through the window. He kisses Faith on the forehead and wakes her up.

"Good morning, beautiful," says Hezekiah.

"Good morning, sunshine," says Faith.

They both shower, get dressed, and ready for the day.

"Are you ready to talk to the pastor today about what we discussed last night?" asks Faith.

"Yes. I just hope he will agree to it. Being in the middle of an outbreak, he might not be so willing."

The happy couple get together and leave the house. Hezekiah opens the Jeep door for Faith, and she jumps into the driver's seat. He takes the passenger seat, and they drive off. Hezekiah stares out the window. He blinks, closes his eyes, exhales, and his head tilts forward.

A truck drives into their lane and slams into their car! Hezekiah jerks and awakens.

"Hezekiah, are you okay?"

"Yeah." Hezekiah scratches the back of his head. "I didn't realize that I fell asleep."

"Was last night too much for you, baby?" she giggles.

Hezekiah glances at her and smiles.

"There is something on my mind that I've wanted to ask you," asks Faith.

"What?"

"Why am I the only one driving everywhere? I've been driving us around a lot. I don't mind, but why don't you ever volunteer to drive?"

Hezekiah grins and chuckles. "Because I don't have a license."

"You don't have a license? I don't believe it," says Faith. She chuckles. "How did this happen?"

"Well, when you're royalty, you don't need to drive. I was driven around everywhere. And with everything that I've been through, I never had time to get one."

"I'm going to not only teach you how to drive, but I'm going to personally make sure you get your license."

A white flash catches Hezekiah's attention. He turns his head toward the window. The hairs on the back of his neck stand on edge. A spirit sprints across the sidewalk, keeping pace with the car. Hezekiah turns his torso toward the window.

"Hezekiah, what's wrong? What do you see?"

Hezekiah grits his teeth.

"I'm a big girl; I can handle whatever it is. What do you see?" asks Faith. She puts her hand on his leg to calm him down.

He's hesitant but gives in. "I see a spirit keeping pace with the car."

"Is it doing anything?"

"No. Just keeping pace."

Faith glances out the window and sees nothing. Glancing at Hezekiah, she notices his muscles tensing. Normally, it sends her emotions on a wild ride, but her shoulders tense and stiffen. The spirit runs off into another direction. Hezekiah relaxes.

Minutes later, the couple arrives at the church. Hezekiah gets out first and scans the area. He opens the car door for Faith, and they go inside the church. They walk to the pastor's office, hand in hand. The pastor and his wife walk out of the office.

"Hey, here's the happy married couple. How are you two doing today?" asks Brian.

"We are doing great, Pastor. How are you?" asks Hezekiah.

They walk into the office. Brian and Lisa stare at them, chuckling.

"So, how was the honeymoon?" asks Brian.

"And what did you do?" asks Lisa.

Oh, here we go, think Hezekiah and Faith.

Faith opens her mouth, and Hezekiah starts talking. "We went to the beach and had a good time talking to old friends and work colleagues."

"That sounds like a wonderful trip. What beach did you go to?" asks the pastor.

Faith is impressed that Hezekiah can instantly take charge of a situation. She smiles and sits back in her chair.

"We went to the City of Light," says Hezekiah.

"Oh, the sand and ocean shore there are so beautiful," says Brian.

"Yes, it is."

"What else did you do?"

"We also went to a nice restaurant and reflected on old times with old friends."

"Where did you go after that, and what did you do?" asks Lisa with a slight chuckle. Faith frowns.

"Look, lady, we're not telling you what we did in the hotel room. You can just forget it," says Faith out loud, not meaning to.

Both Brian and Lisa smirk, chuckle, and laugh from their gut.

Faith and Hezekiah blush. Both the pastor and Lisa suck in breath. Their faces turn red. They fall to their sides and struggle to hold the chair handles.

"Oh, that was rich. I'm sorry," says Brian, cackling and catching his breath. "We just ask this question of all the couples we marry to see what they do. This, by far, was the farthest we pushed someone."

"You two must have had a really good time with each other to feel so much pressure," says the pastor's wife, and she bursts out laughing again.

Hezekiah and Faith sit there, blushing. The pastor and Lisa calm down.

"You don't know this, but we also ask these questions to gauge how a newlywed couple is doing."

"Oh, for what reason?" asks Hezekiah.

"So that you can get better counsel. We just started a program where a professional marriage counselor comes in and advises young married couples to make sure that their marriage stays strong for life."

"That's a good Idea, Pastor, thank you," says Hezekiah.

"When do we have these sessions?" asks Faith.

"Every week. It could be one of you or both of you at the same time. But both of us will be here to listen. Don't worry. The sessions will always be confidential. We even have a psychiatrist if need be."

"Okay. That sounds great," says Faith. She glances at Hezekiah.

"Before we leave for band practice, we needed to talk to you about something," says Hezekiah.

"What is it?" asks Brian.

"I've been wondering... how has church attendance been around here? Before the outbreak, of course."

"Well, we see good numbers, I suppose, but I don't think we're performing as well as we could. But that's with any church."

"I was thinking about the invasion and how people were glad to be safe, but not a lot of people turned their lives over to God."

"That's not necessarily true. We've had a lot of reported salvations in the church recently."

"That's in the church. I'm talking about the entire city."

"We don't think we can reach the entire city or fit everyone from the city in the church," says Brian.

"That's where I disagree. When I was in the City of light, I witnessed an entire city receive Christ."

Pastor Brian squints his eyes. "What? How is that even possible?"

"With God, all things are possible. The people saw the need to get saved after their ordeal, and they took it. Anyway, I was thinking that with everything going on, the church could step in and have a revival," says Hezekiah. He studies the pastor's face. It fluctuates between a smile and frown.

"We can't do that. There is an outbreak going on. If we expose people to the virus that's taking place, it will cause a lot more people to get sick."

"God is the one who decides who lives or dies."

The pastor frowns and shakes his head. "Why do you want to do this revival in the middle of an outbreak? Are you trying to bolster your own name?" he says, hands trembling.

"I, no... I just want to help," says Hezekiah. Hezekiah leans back in his chair.

"I'm sorry, Hezekiah. I'm just not sure that God... I'm not sure that I'm comfortable with that. I don't want people coming in here and getting the whole congregation or my wife sick. I just can't..."

Lisa puts an arm around her husband's shoulder. "I'm sorry, Hezekiah, but we are kind of new to the Christian faith ourselves. I don't think we can do something like that yet. Let us pray about it first."

"Well, maybe we can have the revival online," says Faith.

The pastor's face brightens. "That's a great idea! Everyone is afraid to leave their homes, so we can bring the church to them! We can start setting things up today to prepare."

Hezekiah glances at Faith and smiles. Her heart skips a beat.

The group gets up and makes their way to the auditorium.

Chapter 38

HIDDEN DANGER

AS THEY MAKE THEIR WAY TO THE AUDITORIUM, Faith grabs Hezekiah's arm and the touch sends warmth through his body. They make it to the theater. The band sets up their instruments and prepares for practice. A few songs for the upcoming Sunday has already been prepared, but the sudden outbreak casts uncertainty on this Sunday's attendance. Everyone greets each other, and Hezekiah makes his announcement about the revival. The band members are hesitant. No one wants to get sick. Faith tells them most of the revival will be online, and their fear turns to joy.

They go over a list of songs to decide which ones to sing for the revival. The happy couple settles for a duet. They take about thirty minutes practicing the words, rhythm, and melody. Hezekiah sings his part first.

His smooth tenor voice echoes. His voice goes into slight vibrato. Faith starts singing. Her smooth voice begins with vibrato as well. The band joins in, carrying the melody. A flash enters the corner of Hezekiah's eye. The other singers join in. Faith sings and glances at Hezekiah. His body is stiff and his muscles tense. He moves his head left and right.

Sandra, one of the backup singers, sings over Faith's part.

Faith and Sandra compete for vocal dominance, and Hezekiah's voice flattens. A spirit in the front row stares at him. The drummer competes with the guitarist. Hezekiah spots another spirit in the room, going from one performer to another.

"You're better than she is. Why don't you have the lead vocal on this song? You should prove yourself. Sing louder," says the evil spirit to Sandra.

The spirit travels to the guitarist. *"It's time to shred. This song calls for a guitar solo. Do it now, and they'll be impressed."* The guitarist shreds on his guitar.

The spirit travels back to the drummer. "Don't let the guitarist out-shine you. You are the one who carries the rhythm in this band." The drummer starts a solo.

The evil spirit on the front row pulls out a sword and leaps toward Faith. Hezekiah leaps off the stage. In midair, he summons the sword of the Spirit, twirls, and overhand strikes, but the evil spirit flies backward. Hezekiah follows through with a spinning kick. The demon disappears as his foot slams into the chair, and it breaks in half.

Everyone stops rehearsing. Hezekiah glances around the room. He hears whispers and scans the room for the evil spirits.

"Maybe we should end things here," says the guitarist named Mike.

"I agree," says Sandra.

The entire band exits the auditorium. Faith is standing on stage, staring at Hezekiah, her face turning red.

"Faith, are you okay?" asks Hezekiah, still scanning the room. She doesn't say a word. "What's wrong?" *She must be traumatized,*

"Faith, don't worry, I will protect you."

"Protect me from what?" asks Faith. Her eyebrows drawing together. "What do you mean?"

"Hezekiah, you just attacked something that wasn't there."

"What?" asks Hezekiah. "No, no, no. There was an evil spirit dressed in white that lunged at you with a sword."

"Is that what you saw?" says Faith, She blinks a few times and shakes her head. *Is Hezekiah going crazy?* "We didn't see that. What we saw is you attacking the air and plowing into a chair."

"Huh?"

Hezekiah bows his head and turns his gaze at her. Faith's heartbeat slows and she lowers her gaze. *Oh, Hezekiah.*

"I must have embarrassed you. I'm sorry." says Hezekiah. Faith's eyes water. Hezekiah's head bows, and he walks toward the door. She jumps off the stage and runs after him.

"Hezekiah, wait!" she shouts. He stops but doesn't turn around. She touches his shoulder gently, causing warmth to cascade across his body. She turns him around, lifts his head, and peers into his eyes. "I don't know what's going on, but I'm here for you, for better or for worse."

Hezekiah smiles. "I know this looks bad, but I saw an evil spirit lunge at you. Which is why I reacted the way I did."

"We can all see monsters and demons in plain sight. Why is it that we can't see the ones you're fighting?"

"I don't know." *Could I be going crazy?*

"Let's just go home," says Faith.

"But don't we have to tell the pastor?"

"Let's not worry about that right now. You need some time off. I'll call the pastor and tell him you don't feel well."

As Faith holds his arm, they both exit the auditorium and leave the church. Meanwhile, the band members conduct a meeting with the pastor.

Chapter 39

INVISIBLE ENEMY

HEZEKIAH AND FAITH WALK TO THE JEEP AND GET in. Faith starts to drive. They leave the church and drive onto the road. Both sit thinking to themselves as the hum of the street enters the Jeep. Faith glances at Hezekiah. His eyes water, and he bows his head. Faith exhales.

From the church roof, the evil spirit Murder scans the road for Faith's Jeep. *There you are.* Murder swoops down and catches up to the Jeep. He swoops down, flying on the passenger side. A shining light hits the corner of Hezekiah's eye. Hezekiah turns his head. Murder waves at him. Hezekiah's muscles tense. Faith glances at Hezekiah and notices his muscles tensing. She peeks out his window but sees nothing. She puts her hand on his leg and rubs it. He exhales. Murder smiles wide and furrows his brow.

"What's wrong, Hezekiah? Can't get a grip?!" asks Murder.

"I don't know why I'm worried. You're not even real," says Hezekiah.

"Who are you talking to?" asks Faith.

"Oh, I'm real. You're about to find out how real I am!"

Murder rams the car, and the Jeep swerves. Faith fights the wheel and regains control.

"Oh, look ahead, or you're dead. I wouldn't want you crashing into someone," says Murder.

Hezekiah turns his head to the road. A dark angel stands in the road a yard from the Jeep. it stares at Faith. Hezekiah grabs the wheel and yanks it to the left. The Jeep swerves away from the angel.

"Hezekiah, what are you doing!" shouts Faith. She yanks the wheel to the right and steadies the Jeep into her lane. Hezekiah turns his head toward the passenger window and stares.

"Oh, look, there it is again," says Murder, pointing.

Hezekiah jolts his head toward the street. Another dark angel stands in the middle of the street, seconds away from the Jeep. He yanks the wheel again. The Jeep swerves out of the way of the angel and toward an oncoming car. Faith screams and yanks the wheel. The Jeep swerves back into her lane.

"If you're going to do this, get out!" shouts Faith.

Murder pulls out a sword. Hezekiah takes off his seat belt. He presses a button, and the convertible top pulls back.

"Hezekiah, what are you doing? I didn't mean it," says Faith.

Hezekiah crouches in the seat. Murder swoops above the Jeep and dives down. Murder draws his arm back and swipes. Hezekiah blocks. Air whooshing around him, he struggles to keep his balance.

"Hezekiah!" shouts Faith.

The dark angel looks at Faith. He flies backward, thrusts around the Jeep, and zooms in on Faith. Hezekiah leaps out the Jeep and counters him. They miss an oncoming car. They fly through a field, slam onto, and roll across the soft grass in the park. They spring to their feet. Murder swipes, and Hezekiah counters. They clash swords multiple times in the low grass. Faith looks back in her rear-view mirror, and Hezekiah is fighting the air.

Murder thrusts backward and flies off to chase Faith. Hezekiah speeds off in pursuit. The angel spots the Jeep. Hezekiah leaps into the air and hits Murder in the back. They fly toward an oncoming tractor trailer. Hezekiah and Murder twist and slam onto the top of the trailer. They slide and roll across the top to a stop. Both Murder and Hezekiah stand. Hezekiah is on the back edge of the trailer.

Murder zooms at Hezekiah and swipes. Hezekiah counters and pushes murder backward. Murder thrusts and swipes to cut him in half. The man of God blocks. Hot sparks fly. Murder pushes him back to get him off the truck. Hezekiah spins out of the way. Murder flies off the truck, turns in midair, and rockets toward Faith's Jeep. Hezekiah zooms off the truck. Murder shoots toward Faith. He points his sword toward her. Murder zeros in. Hezekiah shoves Murder away and into a building. Hezekiah lands on the hood of the Jeep. The Jeep slightly swerves. Faith keeps driving and closes the convertible top. Instead of heading home, she drives to her father's house. Murder watches from a distance and laughs.

Chapter 40

REVELATION

FAITH MAKES IT TO HER FATHER'S STREET. HEZEKIAH is on the hood of the Jeep. Frank is about to open the front door. He turns around. His daughter and Hezekiah pull up in the Jeep. Hezekiah jumps off the hood of the vehicle, and Faith gets out of the Jeep. He takes hold of Faith's hand. They walk toward the house, she stops, making him stop. She stares him in the eyes.

"Hezekiah, what happened today?"

"What do you mean?"

"You were fighting something that wasn't there."

"Didn't you see that angel trying to kill you?"

"No!" She puts her hands up and exhales. She touches his arm. *Is Hezekiah crazy? Was he really fighting someone? Is my life really in danger?* Her hands reach up and cup her face. She exhales. Hezekiah puts a hand on her shoulder and pulls her close. Faith buries her head in his chest and holds him. Tears stream down her face. She pulls back and gazes into his eyes. Faith's eyes are bloodshot. Hezekiah caresses her hair. They let go and walk toward the house.

"Is everything okay?" asks Frank.

"Dad, we have a problem," says Faith.

They walk into the house and sit down in the living room by the coffee table.

"So, what's going on?" asks Frank.

She looks at Hezekiah, and he nods.

"Well, what is it?" asks Frank.

"Hezekiah is fighting against evil spirits that we can't see," says Faith.

Frank's eyes open wide. "How long has this been going on, and does anyone else know?"

"We don't know," says Faith.

"Let's start with today. What happened today?"

"While we were rehearsing, Hezekiah leaped off the stage, sliced the air with his sword, and did a flying spinning side-kick to one of the chairs in the auditorium," says Faith.

"Oh my. Uh, Hezekiah, what did you see that prompted you to do that?"

"I saw an evil spirit leap toward Faith to attack her. I countered his attack, and he disappeared for a while," says Hezekiah.

"That wasn't the only thing that happened," says Faith. "Before we got to the church, Hezekiah said he saw something keeping pace with the car. I didn't see it. However, after we left the church, Hezekiah saw something, and the car felt like it was bumped. Hezekiah then grabbed the wheel and yanked it. I pulled it back, and he yanked it again."

Frank frowns. "Hezekiah, why did you yank the wheel?" asks Frank.

"The evil angel pointed ahead. I looked and saw another angel standing in the middle of the street, staring at us. So, I yanked the wheel to move the car out of the way. It happened a second time, and I did the same thing," says Hezekiah.

Frank strokes his chin. "Okay. Faith, you didn't see any of this, am I correct?"

"No, Dad, I didn't," says Faith.

"What else happened?" asks Frank.

"I screamed at Hezekiah to get out of the car. He unbuckled his seat belt and crouched in the seat. He jumped up and pulled out the sword of the Spirit. He was shielding himself. After that, he jumped out of the car. I looked back and saw him fighting the air in the park across the street."

"Hezekiah, is it safe to say you were fighting someone?"

"Yes," he responds.

"Okay, I think I know what's going on."

"What?" both Faith and Hezekiah say in unison.

"Hezekiah is fighting something we can't see," says Frank.

"Dad, I don't mean to sound disrespectful, but I think we established that."

"Let me explain further. There is a story in the Bible where a prophet named Balaam was hired by Moab to curse the children of Israel. Anyway, after much coaxing by Moab, Balaam went to do it. Riding his donkey, an angel of the Lord appeared on the road with a sword drawn in his hand. Numbers 22:23 states: 'When the donkey saw the angel of the LORD standing in the road with a drawn sword in his hand, it turned off the road into a field. Balaam beat it to get it back on the road.'"

"Are you saying that Hezekiah sees demons we can't?"

"That's exactly what I am saying," says Frank. Hezekiah exhales. "Hezekiah is the Spirit Warrior. Everything he does, heck, everything we do, because we are children of God, is linked to the spirit world. Beyond that, everything people do is linked to the spirit world. I'm not saying that all people who see things are not crazy or that they are. What I am saying is that in Hezekiah's case, he is seeing angels who are hiding from us."

Faith hugs Hezekiah. "I'm sorry." She kisses his forehead and lets go.

"It concerns me because we can't see the enemy we could see before. We'll just have to rely more on God to keep us safe," says Frank. His phone goes off. He glances at it. "Oh, no, I have to go back to the hospital. I'll take my leave now. Feel free to lock up if you go."

———————◆———————

Meanwhile, Pastor Brian is talking with the band members and the psychiatrist about Hezekiah at the church.

"So, you're telling me that Hezekiah did all of this to the air?" asks the psychiatrist.

"Yes," says Sandra.

The pastor frowns and glances at his wife.

"Maybe we should take Hezekiah off the team," says Sandra. The band members agree.

"What do you recommend, Doctor?" asks the pastor.

"Let's get him to come in, and I'll take it from there. If things are as bad as you say, he may have to be committed to the hospital for a while," says the psychiatrist.

Chapter 41

PROFESSIONAL "HELP"

THE NEXT DAY, HEZEKIAH AND FAITH AWAKEN IN her father's house. The night before, Faith and Hezekiah cleaned and sanitized the house. She cooked a few meals and placed them in the fridge for her Father. Hezekiah and Faith get ready to go to the church. A phone buzzes on the dresser. Hezekiah answers the phone.

"Hello? Hey, Pastor, how are you doing?" asks Hezekiah.

"I'm doing well."

"So, is everything okay?"

"Yeah. Before rehearsal today, we need to have a meeting with you."

"Okay. We'll be there in a few minutes."

"Okay. See you then," says Brian.

Hezekiah hangs up the phone. "Who was that?" asks Faith.

"That was the pastor. He wants to have a meeting."

"Is it about what happened yesterday?"

"I bet."

"What are you going to do?" asks Faith.

"I'm going to tell him the truth." They walk out the room and toward the front door.

Faith takes hold of his arm. "What if he doesn't believe you?"

"I don't know, but I know that God is with me." He smiles. "Are you with me?"

"Of course, I'm with you! I love you. You're my husband," says Faith, smiling. "I'm with you 'til death do us part.'"

Hezekiah squints at the negative thought. He holds Faith's hand, and they walk out the door and head to church.

———————❖———————

Several minutes later, Hezekiah and Faith arrive at the church. They walk inside, and the pastor greets them. They walk to the pastor's office. Brian opens the door and Henry, the psychiatrist, sits in the pastor's seat. Hezekiah and Henry exchange greetings and sit. Henry's curly gray hair matches his black-framed glasses.

Hezekiah," says Henry, "About what happened in the auditorium yesterday. I want to know what happened, in your words."

Tempted to lie, Hezekiah gulps. "We were rehearsing, and I saw an evil spirit attack Faith."

"You saw an evil spirit attack Faith, you say?" Henry rubs his gray beard.

"Yes. I also saw another evil spirit talking to the people on stage, whispering in their ears, telling them to be jealous of each other," says Hezekiah.

"I see," says Henry. "Have you seen this evil spirit at any other time yesterday?"

"Yes, it tried to attack us the other day. I fended it off, and we made it home."

"Okay. Faith, did you see this evil spirit?"

Faith leans backward in her chair and puts her hand on her chin as she squints.

"It's okay, Faith, you can tell the truth," says Hezekiah above a whisper.

"No," says Faith audibly.

"No, you're not going to tell the truth, or no, you didn't see anything," says Henry with a cackle, glancing at the pastor.

Hezekiah holds up his hand. "Hold on there. Don't accuse my wife of being a liar," he says with a sharp voice.

"Okay. No one is accusing your wife of anything," says Henry, slightly putting a hand up. "We just want to find out the truth."

Hezekiah's muscles slightly tense. His mind formulates more responses, but Faith puts her hand on his shoulder and slowly caresses it. The fact Hezekiah can stand up for her in regular conversation puts a smile on her face.

"To answer your question, I didn't see the evil spirit, but Hezekiah has fought against a lot of strange foes before; this is just a new one," says Faith.

"Hezekiah, how many battles have you been in?" asks Henry, putting his hand on his belly.

"I've been in a lot of fights. Some involving people, others involving demons."

"Like the fight you had with Mr. Warrington?" says Brian with a teeth-baring smile.

"Yes, like the battle I had with Mr. Warrington, who turned out to be Warlord," says Hezekiah.

"Do you have nightmares about the battles you've been in?" asks Henry.

"Yes, sometimes."

"Do you have fears about Faith being killed?"

"Yes," says Hezekiah. He glances at Faith. "But then I remember that Faith's life is in God's hands, not mine."

"Have you ever hallucinated during a fight?"

Hezekiah exhales. "Yes."

"Really? Does this often happen?" Henry asks, leaning forward slightly.

"No," says Hezekiah, slightly lowering his eyebrows. "This only happened when I was fighting against the dark angel Deception."

"So, no hallucinations after that?"

"No."

"Okay. Well, I think we're done here," says Henry.

"Okay," says Hezekiah. "Can we go to the rehearsal now?"

"Yes, go ahead," says the pastor.

Hezekiah and Faith get up and leave the room. Henry walks them out and watches. They walk off into the distance. Henry returns to the office.

"So, what do you think?" asks Brian.

"I recommend that he seek help immediately. I believe he's having visual and audio hallucinations."

Brian puts his hand under his chin. "What makes you so sure? He fights demons we can see all the time," says Brian.

"That's just it. He fights monsters that we can see. What he's dealing with now is something that's not there. With my experience in dealing with patients having Psychosis—"

"Wait a minute. Are you saying that Hezekiah is crazy?" asks the pastor, frowning.

"I believe he's having hallucinations. I know it can be hard to hear, but this happens to people all the time. And with Hezekiah being the town savior and all, I believe it would be in the city's best interest to make sure that the Spirit Warrior is mentally healthy."

Pastor Brian paces and softly shakes his head. "So, what do we do from here? Does Hezekiah see you every day?"

"Yes, but it has to be in a safe place."

"What do you mean?" asks Brian, squinting.

"Seeing things that aren't there is one thing. Attacking them with a dangerous weapon is something else completely. We need to get Hezekiah to the psychiatric hospital."

Pastor Brian stands up and turns away. He exhales and starts to pace slowly. He turns back to Henry with a frown and exhales. "How are we going to get him to the hospital?"

"Just have him meet you at the hospital. Go there to pray for people, and we'll have another meeting afterward," says Henry calmly.

"What about today? He's about to have rehearsal with other people. If he's really a danger to other people, should he be here today?" asks Brian.

"Since he is so strong, we won't be able to get him to the hospital today without a great deal of force. So just monitor him today, let him feel as if things are normal. If something goes wrong today, just excuse him today. But tomorrow, at the hospital, I'll have my people ready just in case something goes wrong," says Henry. He picks up a stress ball to squeeze.

Chapter 42

VOTE OF NO CONFIDENCE

HEZEKIAH AND FAITH WALK TOWARD THE AUDI-torium. Their hearts pound in their chests. Thoughts of mutiny from the other performers pass through his mind. They enter the sanctuary. The band members are on stage.

"What are they doing here?" asks Mike.

"Excuse me?" asks Hezekiah.

Mike quickly puts his head down.

Sandra throws her hands in the air and paces. "Mike, if you're not going to say anything, I will. After your outburst yesterday, we are afraid to do this rehearsal with you. We were prepared to go on with the revival without you," she says brashly.

"So, what are you saying?" says Faith.

"We are saying that your husband is not mentally stable enough to get through rehearsal," she says, approaching Faith.

"My husband is perfectly stable to take on and run this rehearsal," says Faith sharply.

"After yesterday's performance, I beg to differ. I hardly call leaping off the stage and attacking a chair mentally stable. Besides, we are more than capable of managing ourselves. We were doing this long before you two got here, and we will do this long after."

Her tone of voice and words help Hezekiah see through her resentment. "So, is this what all this is about? You are upset because I was made the worship pastor?"

"That is not what this is about. This is about you jumping off the stage and attacking a chair! But since you brought it up, yeah, I would be a better worship pastor than you! You know what? If you're going to stay here, I'm leaving!" Sandra starts to walk, and the others move to follow her.

"Wait a minute. I'll leave," says Hezekiah. They stop to look at him. "No need to ruin the revival over ego. People's lives are in jeopardy. I don't want to be a hindrance for what God is trying to do in this church." He motions to Faith, and they both leave the room.

They pass the time by helping other pastors in the church. At the end of the day, they leave for home. On the way home, Hezekiah is quiet. Faith glances at him. He's staring out the window. She puts her hand on his leg. Hezekiah turns his head and smiles. She can still see the sadness in his eyes.

"Let's not give up. I'm prepared to work on the song at home if you are," says Faith.

Hezekiah's face brightens. "Thanks. I would really like that."

"Let's start as soon as we get back." Instead of going home, they go to her father's house.

Once they get there, they find out that he's not at home. They start to rehearse the song lyrics for the revival, and they practice into the night. Afterward, they go to sleep.

Chapter 43

THE INVASION

HEZEKIAH RUNS ACROSS THE ROOFTOPS OF THE city with the sword of the Spirit in hand. As the sun sets in the sky, the evil spirit Murder runs alongside him. Murder attacks, swiping with his blade. Hezekiah dodges. Hezekiah zips backward and strikes with a blast of light. Murder dodges and counters with his sword. Clashing in combat, a myriad of evil laughter echoes into Hezekiah's ears. He leaps away from Murder and gazes into the sky. Thousands of evil spirits fly into the city from above. People run from their houses and collapse in the streets. Their skin and muscles shrivel away. Their bones crack and turn to dust. The demons cackle. Hezekiah peers from the roof top and sees Faith outside. She gazes at Hezekiah and starts to wilt before his eyes. She grabs her throat and gasps for air. Reaching for Hezekiah, her mouth goes dry. She collapses to the ground and turns to dust.

"No!" shouts Hezekiah. He awakens from his sleep, breathing heavily. Hezekiah sits.

"What's going on!" shouts Faith, awakening from her sleep.

Faith gently puts her hand on Hezekiah's shoulder, and he starts to calm down. "It's okay, baby; you can tell me. I can handle it," she says.

Hezekiah tries to smile, but it fades as he tells her the dream from start to finish.

"What do you think this dream means?" asks Faith.

"I think that this virus that is going on is related to the evil spirit I'm seeing," says Hezekiah.

"What makes you say that?" Faith softly rubs his back.

"I don't know, but if I'm right, this virus is going to explode with a lot of new cases very soon."

They both sit together in the quiet room. He peers into her eyes. "I don't want to lose you."

"Don't worry about that," says Faith. She puts her hand on his face and kisses him. The kiss sends warmth through his body. She pulls back a hair's length. "I'm here now, so don't worry about it." She kisses him again, and he starts to sweat. "In fact, let me help you take your mind off things."

Her kisses make his body tremble. Kisses multiply as they lie down. A flush of warmth consumes their bodies in the coolness of the night.

Chapter 44

CAN WE PRAY?

BEFORE SUNRISE, AT THE HOSPITAL, DR. FRANK IS making rounds. He visits the lab.

"How are the blood tests going?" asks Frank.

"Everything is going great," says the technician named Gena.

"What are we dealing with? Is it a single virus, or are multiple viruses hitting this community?"

"It's one virus, but we don't know what it is. I'm sorry we don't have a positive answer for you. The only thing we can confirm is that the virus is airborne. I'll let you know if we find out anything else."

"Keep me posted. I'll call you back within the hour." Dr. Frank walks out of the lab and down the hall toward the elevator. As he strolls through the hall, another doctor comes to him, asking a question about the virus he cannot answer. The doctor walks away, shaking his head.

"Oh God, I need a breakthrough," he prays. "Please help me to solve this problem. If not by my hand, then by Yours, in Jesus's name." He resumes walking and reaches and enters the elevator. A few minutes later, he exits the elevator and walks toward his office. His office phone is ringing off the hook. He picks up the phone.

"Doctor Frank Parker speaking."

"Hello, this is Governor Roxbury. How are you doing, sir?"

"I'm doing okay, Governor. How is everything?"

"I'm personally in a great bill of health, thanks to you all, but the city is still under stress, and I'm starting to see people around me die."

"I know what you mean. If you're calling to see if we've found a solution to the outbreak, we have not. And I'm afraid that the situation is only going to get worse."

"How so?" asks the governor.

"We still don't know what this virus is, and it's now airborne. If we cannot contain this virus, the entire city is in peril."

The governor exhales. "What is Hezekiah doing? What can he do about this?"

"I don't quite know. I've been here so much..."

"Hezekiah is a man of God, is he not?"

"Yes, he is."

"Get him to the hospital and have him pray for people. Maybe God will cure people through him."

"That's not a bad idea," says Dr. Frank, stroking his chin.

"It's better than nothing. And at this point, we have nothing else to work with. Look, Doc, I know you, and you know me, so I can tell you this. I care about the people. You know I do. I am new to Jesus. I heard that He did this whole thing all the time, didn't He?"

"Yes, He did, but..."

"That settles it. I'll be there within the hour. Make sure that Hezekiah is there too."

"But Governor, I..."

"You know what? I'll make sure he's there. He works at Central City Church, right?"

"Yes, but..."

"I'll give Pastor Brian a call. Just be ready. Let the rest of the staff know that a group will be touring the hospital to pray for the sick. Okay? Bye." *Click.*

Frank looks up toward heaven. "You must be up to something,"

Chapter 45

"I AM WITH YOU"

HEZEKIAH AND FAITH AWAKEN IN EACH OTHER'S arms. They get up, shower, and are in the process of getting dressed when Hezekiah's cell phone rings. Hezekiah grabs it off the dresser and answers it.

"Hello? Hey, Pastor Brian, how are you?" asks Hezekiah. Faith looks over as Hezekiah is on the phone. "So, you want us to meet you at the hospital today? Not at the church. What about the revival?"

———— ·•· ————

"The revival will go as planned. Just show up at the hospital for now. Okay. I'll see you then," says Brian.

The pastor looks at Henry from his seat and frowns. "He's headed there now. Are you sure this is the best idea?" he asks, leaning back in his chair.

"Yes, Pastor. Don't worry, Hezekiah will be okay," says Henry calmly.

The phone rings again. Brian darts his hand to the phone.

"Hello? Ah, Governor Roxbury, how are you doing?"

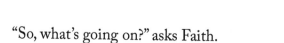

"So, what's going on?" asks Faith.

"We're going to the hospital this morning," says Hezekiah.

"What for?"

"I'm not sure. We'll find out when we get there," says Hezekiah.

They get ready, and he dresses in a white shirt, brown pants, and black shoes. Faith puts on a navy blue dress. They head to the hospital in the early morning, and everything is silent. Traffic is non-existent. As Faith drives toward the freeway, she notices dark clouds coming in from the horizon. She approaches the hospital. A few minutes later, they pull into the parking garage. They park the Jeep and head toward the elevator. The governor's security detail surrounds the elevator. One of the agents has a pack of protective clothing in his hand. Hezekiah and Faith reach the elevator and greets security.

"Please, put these on and come with us," a security staffer says.

What for? Faith thinks to herself.

They put on the equipment and get in the elevator. They travel upward into the hospital. On the main floor, the pace picks up, and they move quickly toward the lobby and check-in.

"What is this all about?" asks Faith.

"The governor is here, and he needs you to help the people," says the chief agent.

"How does he want me to do that?" asks Hezekiah.

"You'll find out when you see him."

The group leaves the main lobby and moves further into the patient areas. They turn a corner and bump into Frank.

"Hey, you two. Glad you could make it," Frank says with a smile.

"What's this all about, Dad?" Faith says.

"Call it a hunch, but I think God is up to something."

They start moving again, and the group enters the emergency room area. People are waiting in the halls. Doctors struggle to care for all the patients. Frank, Faith, and Hezekiah gaze at the scene before them. Hezekiah glances back at Faith. She seems ashen.

"I'm okay, Hezekiah. It's just a little cold in here," says Faith. She starts to shiver.

They walk down the hall and see the governor approach. The governor is dressed in blue scrubs. He joins them, and they walk to a nearby break room to talk.

"I suppose you're wondering why you are here," says Roxbury.

"Yes. I didn't know I would be meeting you here. I was supposed to meet with Pastor Brian." says Hezekiah.

"I talked to him. He will be here later on. It seems that you two have a lot to talk about," says Governor Roxbury.

Oh no, what did he tell the governor? Hezekiah thinks.

"In any case, that does not affect what I want to do now."

"What is it you want to do?" asks Hezekiah.

"I want you to do what Christians do."

"Which is?"

"Pray for the sick. Normally, I would scoff at such an idea, but seeing that we have no way to cure these people, we have no other option. I read in the Bible recently that if the church prays over people and anoints them with oil, it will heal the sick. Is that true?"

"Yes, it's true," says Hezekiah. "As long as the person has enough faith to get well."

"But you're the Spirit Warrior. Can't you make this happen?"

Before Hezekiah could say another word, the Holy Spirit interrupts him.

165

I AM with you.

Without another word, Hezekiah walks off. The governor quickly follows, and everyone else follows him. The man of God walks down the hall in his protective suit. He stops and turns to the group.

"Let me go into the rooms alone, lest anyone of you get into trouble."

"Okay," says the governor.

Hezekiah walks into the first patient's room. There is an older man in bed. His family surrounds him along with two dark spirits. Hezekiah reaches to pull out the sword of the Spirit.

Stop. The beings you see are transporters. This man's time has come. He is about to go to the afterlife, says the Holy Spirit.

"Who are you? And what do you want?" asks his wife, squinting her eyes.

"I want to pray for your husband," says Hezekiah gently.

"I get so sick and tired of you Christians pushing your faith on people and taking advantage of people in their time of need," says the wife.

"But I just want to pray..."

"Get out. Get out. I don't want your Jesus!" says the man brashly.

Hezekiah turns to leave and walks out the room. He looks back. The dark creatures pull the man's soul out of his body and drags him into a portal of fire. He hears the man's soul scream. The man's physical body seizes. Frank rushes into the room, leaving the group.

Hezekiah goes to the next room and finds another family with two dark spirits in the room. He knocks on the door and enters the room.

"No, get out. We don't need your prayers either," says the wife of the woman on the hospital bed.

"Are you sure? I won't take long," says Hezekiah. The dark spirits get ready to take the woman.

"If you don't get out, I'm calling security," shouts the woman in the bed.

Hezekiah leaves. he hears the monitors go off, the soul of the woman screaming, and roaring flames.

Hezekiah enters another room with a woman and her wife. Hezekiah turns to leave, but a strong nudge from the Holy Spirit causes him to stop. *Just because they are gay does not mean they won't hear the gospel.* Hezekiah sees two sets of transporters. Two are dark spirits, and the other two are angels.

God, why do I see two sets?

Because they are both on the verge of death and have a decision to make.

Hezekiah knocks on the door.

"What do you want?" yells the woman in the chair.

"I'm here to pray for you two," says Hezekiah.

"Get out, or I'm calling security!" says the woman. Hezekiah turns to leave.

"Wait! Please wait. I want prayer," says the woman on the bed. She turns to her partner. "Just because you don't want prayer doesn't mean I don't."

Hezekiah comes into the room.

"Sir, I've been seeing dark spirits in here since yesterday," says the woman, trembling. Hezekiah glances at the spirits at the foot of her bed. They both hiss.

"Do you want those evil spirits to go away?" asks Hezekiah.

"Yes, please!" says the lady in the bed. Her wife in the chair rolls her eyes.

"Then pray with me. Say: Lord Jesus, I repent of my sins, and I accept You into my heart as Lord and Savior." The lady prays, and the dark spirits hiss and disappear.

"Oh, thank you so much, sir! I can now rest in peace."

Hezekiah turns his gaze toward the woman in the chair. "Don't look at me; she wanted prayer."

The woman gets up and leaves the room. Hezekiah leaves in the opposite direction. He looks back and sees the dark spirits return and follow her to the restroom. She enters the toilet, and they enter the toilet with her. Hezekiah turns to walk away. An alarm goes off in the restroom, and nurses rush to the restroom.

Hezekiah enters the next room. He sees a lone man accompanied by two dark spirits. He pauses and knocks on the door.

"Hello, may I come in?" asks Hezekiah.

"Sure, I guess," says the man, whose name is Whiley.

His body is full of aches and pains as the virus causes distress to surge like fire through his body.

The Holy Spirit whispers: *You need to fight for this one.*

"I'm here to pray for you," says Hezekiah.

"I don't want prayer; I want to live," says Whiley. He gasps and coughs. Pressure grows around his lungs.

Hezekiah searches his mind for the words to say.

"I don't know why people like you say, 'I'm going to pray for you.' What does that even mean? All of my life, I've heard people say, 'I'm going to pray,' or 'My prayers are with you.' I've even prayed myself from time to time, and nothing has ever happened. Nothing fails like prayer," says Whiley, voice hoarse.

"Let me ask you this: Do you want to be made well?" asks Hezekiah.

"How can I be? I'm on my death bed with that stupid virus that's going around." Whiley gasps and coughs. "No one seems to have a cure for it yet. How would I be made well?"

"In the name of Jesus Christ, get up and be made well!" shouts Hezekiah.

Whiley's face turns red. He jumps out of bed, walks toward Hezekiah, and points his finger in his face. "Now you see here," says Whiley. He stops speaking and takes a breath. His eyes widen. He takes a deeper breath and smiles. He touches his chest, and the pressure is gone. He chuckles and puts a hand over his mouth. A tear rolls down his cheek. "Oh, God, You are real. Thank You, Jesus," says Whiley softly.

Hezekiah smiles.

"Do you want to pray now?" asks Hezekiah.

"Oh, yes sir," Whiley says, crying.

They both pray together, and Whiley accepts Christ into his life. Hezekiah leaves that room, and for the next twenty-five rooms, through the power of the Holy Spirit, Hezekiah heals people. The doctors and nurses murmur among themselves. Their patients with the virus and other ailments get healed through Hezekiah's prayer and touch. The name of Jesus spreads in the hospital. The patients or their families wait in the hall for Hezekiah's prayer. Hezekiah travels to the hospital overflow triage area and starts healing people there. Astonishment grows over the name of Jesus as Hezekiah, through the power of the Holy Spirit, continues to heal people.

Two hours later, many people leave the hospital, showing no signs of the sickness. Others are kept for observation just to make sure they are in a clean bill of health.

Hezekiah, Faith, and the governor stop their tour in a secluded hallway at the hospital and rejoice.

"I can't believe that worked!" says the governor. "We should do this for the whole city!"

"Well, there is a revival that is supposed to take place this afternoon," says Faith.

"I plan to be there," says the governor. His phone beeps. He takes it from his pocket and checks the message. "I have to go back to the office now. An urgent matter has come up concerning the virus that I need to attend to. You two take care and make sure to get people to go to that revival." He turns around and briskly walks away. His security detail follows.

Hezekiah and Faith wave as the governor and his security detail leave.

"Wow, God sure does know how to show Himself strong," says Faith.

"Yes, He does," says Hezekiah. His phone buzzes. He checks the screen. He has several missed calls from Pastor Brian. "Oh, I completely forgot."

"What?"

"We have to meet with Pastor Brian."

"Where is he?"

"Apparently, he had a delay at the church, but now he is at the hospital. He wants us to meet him on the... down here. On this floor," says Hezekiah.

"Where could he be?" asks Faith.

"He is in room 113."

They look for signs on the walls to direct them. They see a sign for the location of the room. They take off the protective gear and follow the signs and head to the room. They walk in. Brian sits in a chair with a weak smile on his face and another chair faces the wall. Hezekiah and Faith enter the room.

"Hey Pastor, what's going on?" asks Hezekiah. They both take a seat.

The red chair turns around and Henry is sitting in the chair. Murder appears alongside him.

Chapter 46

THE EXAM

HEZEKIAH'S EYES WIDEN. THE EVIL SPIRIT LEANS on Henry's chair. Murder smiles at Hezekiah.

"Do you know why we are here, Hezekiah?" asks Henry.

"No, not exactly," says Hezekiah.

Murder moves slightly. Hezekiah's eyes dart to him.

"We are here because, according to the pastor, your behavior as of late is a bit concerning to us."

"In what way?" ask Hezekiah. He exhales, but his body stiffens. His eyes switch from Henry to the evil spirit.

"Since the incident in the auditorium, we've been concerned about your safety."

Murder pulls a dagger from behind the chair. Hezekiah inhales and frowns.

Faith frowns and stares at Henry. "My husband is plenty safe." She glances at Hezekiah, and his eyes are wide and he is sweating. She notices that he's not staring at the doctor, but at the wall. *Oh no,* Faith thinks.

"Let me ask you a few questions, Hezekiah, and be honest with me. Do you sometimes hear voices?"

Murder flips the dagger in the air and catches it. He then continues this motion.

"Do you hear voices, Hezekiah?"

"Of course, I do. I hear yours right now," Hezekiah says sharply.

"Sir, I'm only here to help. No pressure," says Henry.

Murder stops flipping the dagger. "I'm going to gut this man like a fish. Oh, I'm sorry; you're hearing voices, aren't you? If you tell the truth, I'm going to make this worse," says Murder.

Henry peers into Hezekiah's eyes and notices that he is looking toward the wall. "Besides my voice, are you hearing voices right now?"

Murder mimics the psychiatrist to the exact vocal detail. "Go ahead; honesty is the best policy," says Murder, smiling.

"Yes," says Hezekiah. He gulps.

"What are these voices saying?" asks Henry.

Murder frowns his face. "You're a stupid therapist. I hate you," says Murder.

"The voice just insulted you."

"What did the voice say?" asks Henry.

Hezekiah hesitates to answer. "The spirit said, 'You're a stupid therapist. I hate you.'"

The therapist clears his throat. "Well, there is no need for that. Remember, I'm just trying to help you."

Murder moves the dagger to the side of Henry's neck. Hezekiah almost jumps out of his seat. Faith puts a hand on his leg to calm him down.

"The more you speak the truth, the closer I will put this dagger to his neck. Remember, honesty is the best policy!" Murder says with an evil grin.

"Remember, Hezekiah, we are just here to help. Have these voices ever told you to harm anyone?"

"No," Hezekiah says as he exhales.

Murder quickly moves the dagger closer. Hezekiah flinches. Faith rubs his leg to try to calm him, but it's not working. Henry glances behind him and looks back at Hezekiah.

"Hezekiah, do you see someone else in the room?" asks Henry.

"Remember, honesty is the best policy," says Murder.

Hezekiah's skin is damp with sweat. Murder taps Henry's neck with his dagger. Hezekiah flinches again, and Henry flinches backward and puts his palm up. Murder moves the dagger. Henry switches to rubbing the side of his neck.

"My goodness, my neck seems to be sore for some reason," says Henry. He stops rubbing his neck, and Murder moves the dagger back to the side of his neck.

"Remember, honesty is the best policy!" says Murder with an evil glint to his smile.

"Do you see anyone else in the room with us?" asks Henry.

"If you tell the truth, I will make things worse," says Murder.

"Yes," says Hezekiah. His heart thumps in his chest.

Murder whispers in the therapist's ear. "Say to Hezekiah: What does this spirit look like, and do you often see this spirit?"

Hezekiah frowns, and Henry's eyes, for a brief second, glance to the left.

"What does this spirit look like, and do you often see this spirit?" asks Henry.

Hezekiah's jaws drop in disbelief that Henry took so quickly to Murder's suggestion.

"What does this spirit look like?" asks Henry.

"Yeah, Hezekiah, what do I look like?" asks Murder.

"The spirit looks like a man with short white hair, a pale face with lion's teeth, and a white robe."

Faith's eyes widen.

"Ha! Got her!" says Murder.

"You'll never get my wife," says Hezekiah, eyes sharpening.

"Is the spirit talking to you now? What did it say?"

"It says it got Faith.'"

"Tell the truth one more time, and I will kill him. I will stab him. He will die right now with an aneurism if you say one more word," says Murder. "I'll kill Faith, Pastor Brian, and everyone outside this room if you tell the truth one more time."

"You will not touch my wife!" says Hezekiah.

"Hezekiah, calm down. No one is going to touch your wife," says Brian.

Murder throws his voice and speak from all sides of the room, making Hezekiah look everywhere. Murder shouts, and Hezekiah covers his ears.

Faith starts to sweat. She grips the chair.

"You will not touch my wife!" shouts Hezekiah.

"Hezekiah, calm down; no one is going to harm your wife." Henry quietly reaches under the desk and presses a red button. Hospital security check their pagers. They move from their positions to outside the therapist's office.

"Is the spirit making threatening remarks?" asks Henry.

"Yes!"

"What is it saying?"

"It's going to kill you and everyone in the room!"

"I told you what I would do, Hezekiah. Now die, stupid therapist!" Murder pulls his arm back to thrust the dagger, and Hezekiah charges forward and summons the sword of the Spirit.

Faith stands up. Pastor Brian steps in the way. The Spirit sword travels straight through Brian and slices Murder's hand off. Ten muscle-bound security agents burst into the room and yank Hezekiah out.

They quickly put him on the ground outside as fifteen more agents pile on him.

"You cut off my hand! For that, I'm going to kill your wife instead!" shouts Murder.

"This is for your own good, Hezekiah. Don't resist," says Pastor Brian with a frown on his face.

As Henry picks up a tape recorder and starts to speak into it, Hezekiah sees Murder walk toward Faith. Muscles straining, Hezekiah prays out of desperation: "Lord, in the name of Jesus, open their eyes so they see what I see!"

A light flashes, and everyone looks around for a second. The security officers resume trying to restrain Hezekiah.

"Get him in restraints!" says one of the officers.

They hear Faith scream. They all look back and gasp. A pale-faced man with short white hair and lion's teeth is standing in the middle of the room.

"What in the devil?" says Henry. "Is this what Hezekiah's been seeing?"

"So he... was right the whole time?" shouts Brian.

"So, it appears that I've been caught," says Murder, smoothly.

Faith's eyes stream water. "Who are you?" she shouts.

"That's an interesting question. It has a very long answer," says Murder. "But I'll be short. I'm... your demise." He moves toward Faith.

"Get off me!" screams Hezekiah.

They don't move fast enough, and Hezekiah bursts free. The officers bounce in various directions. Hezekiah leaps and strikes just as Murder disappears into the wall and leaves the hospital. Hezekiah turns to his wife.

"Are you okay, sweetie?" asks Hezekiah, touching her face and arms.

"Yes, baby, I'm okay," says Faith with a smile.

"How were you able to see that, and we couldn't?" says Pastor Brian.

"I don't know," says Hezekiah. "He's not the only one I've seen."

A nurse runs to Henry's office, flailing her arms, "Doctor! Doctor! You're not going to believe what's happening all over town.

Chapter 47

OPENED EYES

"WHAT IS IT?" ASKS DR. HENRY, TREMBLING.

"It's all over the news!" says the nurse.

"What's all over the news?"

"Come with me, and you'll see."

The entire group travels to the nearby, tan, break room. There are only a few chairs by the television. Hezekiah secures one for Faith to sit in.

The security staff grumble and complain about being in pain. The nurse shushes them.

"Be quiet. It's about to start," says the nurse.

———————◆———————

The TV screen shows a news reporter standing in the center of town.

"This is Julie with *Central City News*. We are experiencing another catastrophic attack against the city. We are live in the town square as we see strange apparitions flying in and out of people's houses, making them sick. We were originally out here to report the lockdowns and the outbreak, but suddenly strange spirits started appearing everywhere. People are running around out of fear, wondering where the Spirit Warrior, Hezekiah, is." Julie puts her hand against her earphone. "I'm now receiving a message that the governor is hosting a press conference at City Hall. We will turn our television broadcast over to the press conference currently taking place."

The news broadcast switches from Julie to the governor.

"Dear people of our great city. I come to you today under great distress but with great hope. We are under siege yet again, but we can rest assured that God is still with us," says Governor Roxbury.

"Where is the Spirit Warrior!" shouts a reporter. "I thought he was supposed to protect us!"

"You're wrong. God will protect us. But to answer your question, Hezekiah wants everyone to attend the service at Central City Church today."

"How? The entire city can't fit inside of that building," says the reporter.

"We don't have to. Everyone needs to either gather there or attend the service online immediately."

"Why don't we just go into the bunker, like the last invasion?"

"Because these spirits travel through walls. If we go down there, the spirits will follow. The bunkers will be nothing more than a large casket," says Roxbury.

"There has to be another option."

"We just need too—" A flash of light catches Roxbury's attention. He gazes into the sky and gasps.

"Governor, are you not able to answer the question? Governor. Governor?" The reporter follows Roxbury's gaze and stares into the same direction.

Dark clouds in the sky swoop downward like a giant waterfall.

"Why are the clouds doing that?" asks the reporter.

With his gaze fixated on the clouds, Roxbury asks one of his security officers for a pair of binoculars. Roxbury peers into the binoculars and sees within the clouds, ten thousand evil spirits descending onto the city.

"Those aren't clouds. Those are evil spirits charging toward the city," says Roxbury.

The press stops murmuring. Roxbury hands the binoculars back to his officer.

"Everyone listening to this broadcast, please attend the Central City Church service. Get to Central City Church as quickly and orderly as possible. If you can't get to the front, be as close as possible. Or attend online or by radio. God is the only one who can save us from the spirit of Death. May God have mercy on us all," says Roxbury.

The broadcast switches back to Julie.

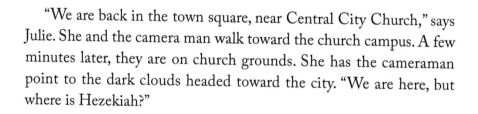

"We are back in the town square, near Central City Church," says Julie. She and the camera man walk toward the church campus. A few minutes later, they are on church grounds. She has the cameraman point to the dark clouds headed toward the city. "We are here, but where is Hezekiah?"

At the hospital, the group all stare at Hezekiah.

"Faith, we have to go now," says Hezekiah. Faith nods. "Pastor, we have to get the revival ready."

"Everything is ready to go. The only people missing are us," says Brian.

"You need to get there as fast as possible."

"Why me? You're the Spirit Warrior."

"People need to see that God is the Savior, not me. So, you need to get there and preach and start praying for people to get well."

"I don't know if I can do that," says Brian.

"You can't, but God can. Through you."

A few minutes later, the entire group leaves the hospital.

Faith drives, and Hezekiah watches the dark mist coming toward the city. She hurries to get to the church before a traffic jam starts. Fifteen minutes later, they are at the church. People have set up the sound equipment outside the church. A sizeable wooden stage has been built. The singers are already there, and the musicians are preparing their equipment. Bottles of oil are on display.

"Who set all this up?" asks Faith.

"I don't know; Pastor Brian?" says Hezekiah, scratching his head.

They both walk up to the stage. He stops and stares at one of the workers setting up the stage equipment. He is a tall man with an athletic frame. He is dressed in a gray hat and gray work suit. Hezekiah stares at him, and the guy smiles and starts working again.

Faith and Hezekiah approach Sandra. "Hey, is everything ready?"

"Yeah, everything is ready," says Sandra. "These people really did a good job. Did you hire them?"

"No. I thought Pastor Brian did."

"About before..." says Sandra.

"Don't worry about it," says Faith.

"No, let me finish. Before your husband came, I was considered for the worship pastor position for the church. When Hezekiah got the job, I got jealous. So, when I thought Hezekiah was having a mental problem, I took advantage of the opportunity to assert myself. For that, I'm sorry."

"We forgive you," says Faith.

Pastor Brian walks up. "You guys really did a good job setting this up so fast. How did you do it?"

"We don't know. We thought you set this all up," says Sandra.

"No, I had everything ready on the inside of the church. I didn't even think or have the time to set up sound and broadcast equipment for the outside. I went to the hospital to meet with Hezekiah." He looks at the workers to see if he can recognize anyone, but he doesn't.

A few minutes later, everything is completely ready, and everyone is ready to perform. The pastor walks up to one of the workers. "Thank you so much for your help. Who are you?"

"Don't worry about that. Worry about what's coming," says the mysterious man as he points toward the horizon. The cloud of darkness is over the city.

Chapter 48

THE REVIVAL

THIRTY MINUTES LATER, THE PLACE IS PACKED with people. People clamor. The band members are behind stage, out of view. The pastor wants them to perform after he says a few words.

The Holy Spirit whispers to Hezekiah's soul: *While on stage, I want you to fight through Me, using your voice. Do not use the physical manifestation of the Spirit sword. It will be a distraction away from Me and put focus on you. Don't use it, no matter what you see.*

"Yes, Lord," says Hezekiah.

Faith walks up to Hezekiah and taps him on the shoulder. "What did God say?"

"Not to fight with the sword."

"What?"

Julie broadcasts live from the crowd. She focuses on the pastor, who is on stage as he begins to speak.

"Welcome to Central City Church! Today, we will go straight to God in prayer." He bows his head. "Dear God, we thank You for everything You have done for us. Thank You for opening our eyes to the true danger that has plagued this city, not trusting in You. So today, we turn back to You, and we pray for your healing hands and protection. In Jesus's name, amen."

Wind gushes from behind the crowd, and they look back and see the clouds entering the city.

"Is someone going to do something!" shouts someone from the crowd. "I should have left the city."

The evil spirits move through the crowd. They touch people, and people start coughing and shaking. Large groups of people run. They try to get away, but the evil spirits block their escape. Some spirits breathe out black smoke from their mouths. Parts of the crowd gag and fall to their knees.

Hezekiah, Faith, Sandra, and the rest of the band emerge on stage. Hezekiah gazes at the enemy spreading sickness. His muscles tighten, and he prepares to leap. *Remember what God said.* He glances at Faith and the rest of the band. The people scream and run. The spirits start punching and kicking people.

"Hezekiah, aren't you going to do something?" asks Mike.

Hezekiah points to Mike. The guitarist softly plays. And Hezekiah softly sings. The others join in. The Holy Spirit moves from the stage into the crowd, and the demons stop attacking. The people up front stare at the stage. The drummer and other musicians join in. The audience turns their focus toward the stage. The demons sneer. As Hezekiah's voice goes into a vibrato, Faith joins in with her smooth voice. The Spirit of God moves from person to person, healing them. People in the crowd start raising their hands, thanking God.

People cheer and clap, and their sickness leaves. Sandra joins in and sings with might. Her soprano voice echoes throughout the crowd. The Spirit of God starts attacking the evil spirits. The dark spirits run and wail. The Spirit of God continues to slay the evil spirits in the crowd. All three singers perform the chorus with power. The audience cheers and sings with the band. Faith and Sandra pull back as Hezekiah begins the second half with a smooth tenor. His voice echoes through the crowd. Faith matches his style and adds more alto.

The evil spirits cover their ears and shriek, tormented by the sounds blessed by heaven. Sandra cuts in, singing with power. All three sing the chorus, and the air electrifies. The audience watching via television sings along, and the evil spirits leave people's homes. The power in their voices builds, and Sandra's voice crescendos with might. All three sing with full strength. In attendance and at home, the audience sings with might, filling the city with the Holy Spirit of God.

The demons retreat and leave the city as everyone worships God. Some of the evil spirits burst into flames, caught by the power of the Holy Spirit. Faith and Sandra soften their voices. Hezekiah smoothly sings his final part as Faith and Sandra join in. They sing in unison until the song's end. The crowd bursts into applause.

In the mountains outside the city, Death watches from a distance and orders the fallen angels into the forest.

"What about the city?" says one of the spirits.

"Remain in the forest and don't worry about the city. I have a plan. Finishing this task is my top priority," says the Death angel. He unfolds his wings, lifts his left arm, and shoots a dark blast toward the city.

Chapter 49

THE FREE OFFER

THE BAND STEPS OFF STAGE AND THE PASTOR approaches the microphone. The crowd is still cheering from the worship.

"Jesus is a healer, as a lot of us have found out today. I'm not going to speak long." The crowd murmurs and quiets down. "In the Bible, in James 5:14–16, it says: 'Is anyone among you sick? Let them call the elders of the church to pray over them and anoint them with oil in the name of the Lord. And the prayer offered in faith will make the sick person well; the Lord will raise them up. If they have sinned, they will be forgiven. Therefore, confess your sins to each other and pray for each other so that you may be healed. The prayer of a righteous person is powerful and effective.' God healed a lot of people here and at home through the music. Now it's time to be cured forever. One day, our lives will end in this world. Unless you are raptured out of here and taken to heaven, you're going to die someday.

"You could be healed during the revival and be hit by a car when you leave. What I'm offering you today is the way to have eternal life. Jesus, the Son of God, died on the Cross to pay for our sins. And He rose from the dead so that we may live forever. If we trust Jesus, no matter what happens today or tomorrow, we will be welcomed by Him when we die. Romans 10: 9-10 says: 'If you declare with your mouth, 'Jesus is Lord,' and believe in your heart that God raised him from the dead, you will be saved. For it is with your heart that you believe and are justified, and it is with your mouth that you profess your faith and are saved.' So, before we leave here today, and you want to accept Jesus Christ as Lord and Savior, then repeat after me."

The audience there and watching by television bow their heads and close their eyes.

"Say: Dear Lord, please forgive me of my sins. I turn away from them now. I accept You into my heart as Lord and Savior."

The people pray with the pastor, and many receive salvation.

"Let's thank God for all that He has done for us," says the pastor.

People in the crowd cheer.

"As we end this revival and as the band comes back on stage, those who want to be prayed for, come up here, and I will pray for you and anoint your head with oil today."

The band, with the exception of Hezekiah and Faith, get back on stage.

"Faith, you were awesome out there!" says Hezekiah.

"So were you!" she says.

"I didn't know we could win a spiritual battle through praising God."

"I didn't either. I guess it's safe to say that we could add the gift of song to our arsenal of weapons of the Spirit," says Faith.

"I guess so."

As the band sings with passion, people come to be anointed with oil. The pastor and the altar staff anoint people's heads with oil. Hezekiah and Faith join in and help. They do this for about an hour. The pastor gives a few closing words and then dismisses the assembly.

From the sky, Central City chopper observes the gathering as the people exit.

Chapter 50

EYE OF THE STORM

"THIS IS JULIE WITH *CENTRAL CITY NEWS*. WE ARE live as the revival has now come to a close. The evil spirits are completely gone from this location. It looks like a miracle has taken place. It also appears, at least from my end, that the sickness that has taken over the city has also disappeared," says Julie. "What is the traffic like leaving the revival, Mitchel?"

"This is Mitchel in Central City chopper; we are reporting heavy traffic leaving the revival."

After the last person leaves, the pastor meets with all the staff in attendance.

"Great job, all of you. God really showed Himself strong through all of you today," says Pastor Brian.

"Good job yourself, Pastor," says Hezekiah.

He looks at Hezekiah. "I would like to apologize for not trusting you. After everything that we've been through, I should have known that you weren't crazy."

"It's okay, Pastor. Don't worry about it."

Faith's phone rings. It's Frank. "Hey, Dad, how are you doing?"

"I have a slight problem," says Frank. "I lost my car keys. Do you have a spare on you?"

"No, I don't, but you have a spare at the house. I'll pick them up."

"Oh, thanks, dear."

"No problem, Dad." Faith hangs up the phone. "I have to go," she tells Hezekiah.

"What happened?" asks Hezekiah.

"Dad lost his car keys. I'll go by his house. I left a spare on the coffee table."

"I'll come with you."

"No, stay here. You have to finish the workday. Besides, the pastor needs your help to dismantle the stage equipment."

"All right. After I'm done, I'll call you."

"Okay. See you soon." Faith moves to leave, and Hezekiah softly pulls her by the hand.

He places his hand on the small of her back, sending soft tingles down her spine. Their eyes meet, and they briefly become lost in each other's gazes. He kisses Faith, and Faith starts to sweat. She exhales. He lets her go.

"What was that for?" she asks.

"Because I love you," he says, smiling.

"I love you too." She pecks him on the lips, then whispers in his ear: "I have a special gift I want you to unwrap tonight." He smiles wider. "Let me go. I'll be back after a while."

Hezekiah watches her leave.

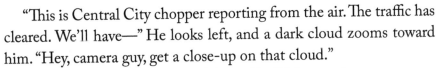

"This is Central City chopper reporting from the air. The traffic has cleared. We'll have—" He looks left, and a dark cloud zooms toward him. "Hey, camera guy, get a close-up on that cloud."

The cameraman zooms in. "Oh my God!" shouts the camera man. His eyes open wide, and his jaw drops. His face pales and his throat constricts.

"What—What is it?!" says Mitchel.

The cameraman points at the cloud. A skeleton wrapped in darkness careens towards them.

"Oh no!" Mitchel glances back at the cameraman and jumps away.

The cameraman withers like a raisin. He falls over dead. Mitchel turns to the pilot, and he's dead.

"Mitchel to Julie! Mitchel to Julie! The spirit of Death is flying toward the city! I repeat, he's—"

The chopper is hit.

"Mayday! Mayday! We're going down! We're going down!" shouts Mitchel as the chopper goes down in a tailspin.

Chapter 51

STORM SURGE

JULIE AND THE CAMERAMAN RUN TO HEZEKIAH and the other band members, WHO are still putting away the sound equipment.

"Hezekiah! Hezekiah!"

He tries to ignore her. Julie slaps him on the back of the head.

"What?" says Hezekiah.

She points to the sky. "The spirit of Death just entered the city, and the news chopper is going down!"

Hezekiah peers into the sky. God enhances his sight. The chopper is in a tailspin. The Spirit Warrior powers up like lightning. Fire engulfs Hezekiah. Armor starts to form on him. The staff is awestruck. Only halfway transformed, he rockets across the ground and into the air. He lands on a nearby building and runs from rooftop to rooftop. The chopper spins closer toward the ground. Hezekiah rockets into the air. He is hit by a skeleton wrapped in darkness.

"Mayday! Mayday!" screams Mitchel. He sees the ground approaching.

Hezekiah and the skeletal beast clash sword to claw in combat, fighting across the rooftops. The Spirit Warrior strikes it with a blast of light and destroys it. Like lightning, Hezekiah sprints and jumps to meet the chopper.

Mitchel sees Hezekiah in the air and takes off his seat belt. The chopper tilts. The man of God reaches the falling chopper. He reaches for Mitchel's outstretched hand. A gray flash hits Hezekiah, knocking him away. The chopper crashes into the ground and bursts into flames in the middle of the street.

"No!" shouts Hezekiah.

The dark skull-creature attacks, swiping with its claws. The beast sees other people on the street and swerves to attack them. The beast shoots tentacles out of itself, and they attach to the people around it. The beast sucks the life force out of them. People age as the monster drains the life out of them. Hezekiah strikes the beast with a blast of light and destroys it. The man of God peers into the sky. Another dark cloud in the sky moves like a comet, headed his way. The Spirit Warrior sprints and jumps high. In the air, he sees it's another skull creature. Before it can fully extend itself to fight, Hezekiah strikes it with a blast of fire, and it bursts into pieces. Hezekiah sees another one coming from the same direction, then two more head his way. As soon as his foot touches the ground, the man of God zips like lightning across the ground. He leaps back to the rooftops of the city and races across them. He leaps in the air and slices with a blast of lightning. With a single stroke, he destroys all three beasts. Hezekiah sprints in the direction they came from.

———————◆———————

Faith arrives at Frank's house. She opens the door, enters the house, and walks into the living room. Faith scans the coffee table for her father's extra car keys. *Here they are.* She grabs them and turns around. A hand slaps her across the face. She tumbles onto her back. Faith holds her face and gazes at her attacker. She gasps, and her heart thumps against her chest. Murder, the evil spirit, is standing over her.

———————◆———————

At the hospital, Frank scans his desk and under the desk. He walks into the lobby.

"Are you looking for these?" says a nurse, dangling a set of keys.

"Yes. How did you find them?" asks Frank.

"I guess you dropped them on the ground."

"Thank you, miss. You are a real lifesaver."

Frank leaves. The nurse's eyes flash a demonic red. She watches Frank.

He walks out the door and calls Faith. He doesn't get an answer. He calls again, and still no answer.

"That's odd," he says. He goes to his Jeep.

———————◆———————

Hezekiah sprints into the warm, green, forest, blazing up the mountain trail like a rocket. Demons align his path way in the woodland.

They back away from him and smile. The trees get smaller, and the rocks get bigger the farther he sprints up. Hezekiah passes the last tree and sprints toward the top of the hill. Hezekiah sprints to the top and slides to a stop. Hezekiah scans the area atop of the mountain. Hezekiah glances upward, and a dark cloud descends from the sky. The black cloud slams into the ground and flows across the ground. Hezekiah's heart thumps against his chest wall. A tall-cloaked figure emerges from the cloud. Its bone fingers grip a gunmetal scythe. His skeleton face peeks from underneath his black hood. The figure peers into Hezekiah's eyes. Death lifts a hand and shoots black lightning. The lightning crackles and surges. Hezekiah is hit by the black lightning, and it scrapes across his body. Breath escapes his body, and pressure compounds into his chest. Hezekiah flounders. The lightning surge stops. Hezekiah falls to his knees. His body smokes.

"You think you could really defeat me, Hezekiah?"

Hezekiah lifts his head and stands. Gritting his teeth, he frowns. "I've fought you before in the City of Light and won. I can do it again," says Hezekiah.

"Oh, really? You are sadly mistaken. I am not the version of death you faced before. See, before, when you fought me at the prison, I was only at one-fourth of my strength. I had multiple jobs to do at different locations, so I was spread thin. I was not expecting to fight against someone like you in the middle of a prison. So when we fought, I lost. But now, knowing full well who you are, I decided to take a different approach."

The black lightning sparks around Death's body, and He shoots Hezekiah. The Spirit Warrior is hit. Hezekiah screams, and his hair turns gray.

"I decided to come at you with 80 percent of my power, but sadly, that may be overkill." The voltage increases. Hezekiah stumbles to his knees, screaming.

Hezekiah's muscles rupture. Blood builds under his skin layer. Death stops shooting, and lightning surges around his scythe. Hezekiah is on the ground, moaning. He pushes himself off the ground and stumbles to his knees.

"I am so powerful, I'm barely considered an angel. I'm considered a concept or an idea," says Death. He glides toward Hezekiah. "But I assure you, I am very much a person." He shoots Hezekiah. Lightning rips through his body. "My power rivals that of Satan himself. I'm quite easily the most powerful entity ever created!"

Hezekiah screams. His skin wrinkles from head to toe. His muscles gradually disappear as his hair falls out. Hezekiah puts his arm in front of him to shield him from the lightning. A barrier forms around Hezekiah's arm, and the lightning surges around it.

"You are only a created being, you are not God," says Hezekiah. The belt of truth sparkles around his waist. The black lightning continues to surge around Hezekiah as he shields himself.

"You think that armor can save you? You're not even worthy to possess it," says Death. The lightning blast hits a few trees in the distance, and they wilt away.

"God is my righteousness." The breastplate of righteousness fully forms around his torso. In conjunction with the sword, it forms armor around his arms, forearms, and hands. The breast plate starts the healing process.

Death stops his attack completely. Hezekiah stands with his arm up as the armor heals him.

"I would love to have a full-on battle with you, but I surrender," says the Death angel.

"What?"

"I surrender. You win. I'll even let the armor fully heal you."

Hezekiah stands there with his arm still up, shielding himself. Two minutes later, the armor restores Hezekiah's youth and hair.

"Aren't you going to ask?" Death says.

"Ask what?"

"Why I surrendered."

"No."

"Humor me."

"Okay, why?" asks Hezekiah.

"It's not your time to die. Not here and not in this way."

What does he mean by that? And why is he stalling? Death glances at his arm as if he's wearing a watch.

"Then why are you still here?" says Hezekiah.

Death says nothing. Two minutes pass by. *What is this guy up to?*

The swordsman's battle injuries are now healed. Two more minutes pass by, but Death is still there. Now he's not even paying attention to Hezekiah. Death is looking down and turning is gaze toward the city.

God, what's going on?

God doesn't answer.

"Aren't you going to ask?" asks Death.

"Okay, what are you doing?" Hezekiah drops his guard, and the armor disappears from neck to toe.

"I'm stalling so Murder can take care of her," says Death.

Hezekiah gasps. "Faith!"

"Yes, now you know. I lured you out here so that I could kill her. I have an agent already at her father's house now, ready to kill her. You fell right for it.

Hezekiah turns to run, but the armor of God won't reactivate.

"Wondering why you can't summon any of your armor? Because I tired you out. The armor healed you. And once you didn't need it anymore, it went away. Because of that, you won't get there in time to save Faith. As it so happens, it's her appointed day to... die."

"No!"

"Unless of course you get there on time," says Death. He starts to laugh.

Chapter 52

UNWELCOMED GUEST

FAITH BACKS AWAY AND GETS UP. "HOW LONG have you been here?"

"I've been here for a while. I figured you would come back sooner or later."

"Have you been following me?"

"Of course, I have."

"How long?"

"I've been following you since your little beach trip."

Faith's eyes widen. "You were the reason I almost got hit by a car?"

"Bingo! I didn't think you would figure that out, but you did. Bravo, dear girl. Bravo," says Murder as he claps his hands.

"What else did you do?" says Faith, hands shaking.

"Oh, I thought you would know by now, dear girl. I was the one Hezekiah saw when you were driving to church. I was the one he attacked at the church, and I was the one who attacked him when you were driving down the road."

"What about the forest?"

"What about the forest? Oh, you mean the fight your husband had behind your house? No, that was one of my cohorts. He tried to make you sick by exposing you to the virus at the governor's mansion. But, because Hezekiah healed you at the house, he tried to lure Hezekiah out to kill you. He then botched his whole plan when he tried to kill Hezekiah. He was an idiot to try to fight the Spirit Warrior head on."

"So did you. So does that make you stupid?"

"My, my. You sure are witty now, aren't you? No, I only attacked him half-heartedly to make him look crazy and drive a wedge between you."

"Why?"

Murder strolls toward her. And she walks back.

"Because, my dear girl, I wanted to separate you two."

Faith squints her eyes.

"Why would I want to separate you two, you ask? It's because I can't seem to kill you when he is around," says Murder. "I've done all sorts of things to try to kill you, and as long as he was around, it all came to nothing. I even tried to expose you to the virus, but you just healed as if nothing happened."

"So that's why I felt a little sick at the hospital?"

"Yep. Now that I've got you right where I want you, I can kill you."

"Wait, who sent you?"

"Death. Who else?" says Murder. Faith backs up. "Now, now, deary, no more stalling. Hezekiah is not coming to save you." Murder approaches Faith.

She whimpers a little. "Oh God, please help me."

"God?" says Murder, smiling. "My dearest girl." He zooms toward Faith, grabs her arm, and breathily whispers into her ear. "God is the one who wanted me to kill you."

Lightning surges through murder's arm and travels into Faith. Faith screams.

———————◆———————

Frank pulls up to his house and glances at Faith's Jeep. He goes to the front door and sees it ajar. He slowly opens the door and scans the doorway. The room is dark and still. He creeps through the front door and scans the room.

"Daddy?"

Frank's head moves toward the sound, and his eyes widen. Faith is on top of the coffee table. Frank sprints to her. *Oh my God, Oh my God!* Frank checks her pulse, and it's faint. Her hands are clammy and her face drips with sweat. She's pale. Murder is hiding in the corner, watching.

Frank rubs her shoulder. "Faith? Faith? Are you okay? Faith? Faith?"

"Daddy?" Faith says as she slowly opens her eyes.

"Yes, dear, it's me."

"Daddy, I... I..."

"Don't worry, sweetie; Daddy's here," says Frank, his voice at a high pitch. Heart pounding into his chest, He dials 911.

"911. What's the nature of your emergency?"

"I need an ambulance, ASAP! My daughter is dying, but I don't know why!"

"We have your address. We will be their shortly."

Frank hangs up and holds his daughter's hand. He kneels down beside her. Lord, God! Please, I beg you! Save my daughter!" Tears stream down Frank's face.

A light Frank does not see fills the room. Faith opens her eyes and gazes upward. Jesus is above her and extends a nail-pierced hand. "Come with Me," Jesus says.

Faith's body falls limp on the table, and she exhales. Faith's spirit lifts from her body, and she takes hold of Jesus's hand, and travels into the light with Him.

Chapter 53

THE SPIRIT WARRIOR

FAITH JOURNEYS WITH JESUS THROUGH A TUNNEL of light. They reach the end of the tunnel on the outskirts of heaven. White clouds fill the entrance of heaven. Jesus strolls with Faith through the shiny, pearly gates. The light of heaven sparkles across Faith's skin, and the sparkles fill her with light. Faith's eyes widen, and she smiles from ear to ear as she sees a city of pure gold in front of her.

———————◆———————

Hezekiah sprints down the mountain trail into the forest. Sonic speed unavailable to him, he is irritated with himself as he sprints and leaps down the path. The evil spirits see his advance down the woods and shoot lightning bolts at him. Hezekiah leaps out of the way of each bolt, running and jumping over fallen trees. Lightning surges around him and pounds dirt into the air. The bolts hit trees and pound into the ground. The sparks fly into the air, sparking across Hezekiah's skin. He tucks, rolls, and leaps out the way of lightning strikes. *God, please protect Faith!* Cross-shaped shafts of light strike into the ground all around him and in front of him, blocking his way forward. Hezekiah gasps and slides to a stop. He leaps off the ground, and they explode. In the air, Hezekiah summons the sword of the Spirit and clashes, sword to sword, with an evil spirit.

———————❖———————

Jesus shows Faith the playground for children. He shows her the streets of gold and her own mansion. Jesus opens the outer doors of her mansion. They walk inside. Inside her mansion, she sees a table. Around the table, she sees twelve men and her mother. They cheer for her. Faith's mind empties from all concern and worry as her face shines in the light of heaven.

———————❖———————

Hezekiah sprints down the path. He scans the area ahead, and three evil spirits stand in the middle of the path, with swords drawn. One has on fiery armor from head to toe. Hezekiah frowns his face and grits his teeth. His heart thumps in his chest. He sprints and leaps toward them. He overhand cuts through the armored spirit. He twirls the sword and cuts through the other two. Two more spirits charge at him, one from the front and the other from behind. He thrusts through one and turns with an overhand slash to the other.

Twenty leap out of the woods from all directions to thrust him through. They swarm and try to pile into him. Hezekiah screams. A surge of adrenaline rushes through his body. He overhand thrusts with a burst of wind. The spirits are hit and fly in various directions, but more swarm in to attack. Hezekiah's blade moves like the wind as his arm blurs, slicing through all demons in his path. More come in unrelenting numbers. Hezekiah adds fire mixed with lightning in his attacks as they come from his left and right flank.

Frustration frowns his face, and he overhand strikes with blasts of fire and Ice. They keep advancing with no end in sight. Hezekiah vertically leaps high and bounces off a tree, launching himself through the air. The dark angels quickly pursue. His eyes widen as he grinds his teeth. The Spirit Warrior turns around in midair and overhead strikes them with a blast of wind. Wind slams into them, and the dark angels slam into the ground. Hezekiah lands hard and twists his ankle. He rolls and gets up, running. His armor shoes rematerialize on his feet. Hezekiah picks up speed like a freight train. He runs toward the clearing. Evil spirits are there to block his way. Without slowing down, he strikes with a large flare of fire and blasts through the horde. He rockets through them like a fiery arrow, disintegrating them as he passes by.

A few minutes later, Hezekiah arrives outside of Frank's house and bursts through the front door. He runs to the living room and sees Faith lying lifeless on the table. Hezekiah goes to her. The Spirit Warrior is breathless. Itching gathers in the back of his throat, and his heart beats violently as he sees the frown on her face. He touches her cheek. Her usually warm face is cold and stiff. Hezekiah's head throbs with a hard, pulsating beat.

"No, no, no," Hezekiah says, whimpering. Like prickly fire, pain bursts through his chest and arms, and they tighten. His body shakes as he loses power in his legs. Hezekiah trembles and falls to his knees. His throat goes dry as his eyes fill with tears. Frank looks at him with bloodshot eyes. Hezekiah's eyes turn red as cold tears pour down his warm cheeks. He puts his hands over his face and sucks in the air.

Seeing his wife there, the one he swore he would protect, he loses hope and his will to fight.

"If only I had been here," Hezekiah says in a hoarse voice. "If I had kept wearing the full armor... she would not have died." Like a bag of bricks, guilt sits on his back as its poison seeps into his pain-stricken body.

The evil spirits from the forest surround Frank's house with the command to kill Frank and Hezekiah.

As Faith talks to her mother, Jesus walks up to her with a gold chest.

"Faith, I have a gift for you," He says with a smile.

Maranda peers into Faith's eyes, nods, and lets her go. Faith goes to Jesus, and Jesus opens the gold chest.

"Is this what I think it is?" asks Faith.

"Yes, it's your very own. Do you like it?"

"Yes!" says Faith with a smile on her face.

"Do you want it? And everything that comes with it?"

"Lord, You know I do," says Faith with a chuckle.

"Okay, then pick it up."

Faith lifts up the Sword of the Spirit from the box, and it shimmers with light. Her body fills with power as she makes practice feints with the sword, swiftly moving it through the air of heaven. Jesus waves, and she turns her head in his direction.

"Now, Faith. I'll explain your gift in detail later; for now, you have to return to earth,"

"But why? I love it here," she says with a smile.

You have to go to earth to save Hezekiah."

"Why can't you bring him here to be with me?"

"Because you two have much work to do on earth. Many souls hang in the balance, and I want you to help Me help them secure a place in heaven with Me."

"Okay, Lord," says Faith.

"Now go." Jesus moves His hand out.

Faith moves away from Jesus's presence, flying through the tunnel back to earth. Her hair and robe majestically flow as she descends from the tunnel back to the earth's atmosphere and flies through the clouds.

"Oh no, she's coming back," says Murder.

"Don't let her come back. Stop her. Stop her!" shouts Death.

A hundred demons swarm toward her. Faith powers up her new fire sword. She strikes the first few as they try to stop her. More jet toward her from below. Faith slices through them with blunt force as she moves faster than the wind. She jets, weaves, and slices through more dark angels, making her way back to her body. More dark angels jet toward her with swords of their own and attack. Faith forays the evil spirits with flashes of fire. Her arm blurs as she downward spins her sword, slashing through each spirit, continuing her descending assault. A massive group of dark angels charges to thrust through her. She slashes with a crack of lightning. The burst flashes through the spirits and cracks with thunder, incinerating the group in the blast.

Seeing that they're getting nowhere, the rest of the evil spirits form an air blockade above the roof of Frank's house, with Murder in the center. Faith grits her teeth. She puts her sword away and raises her forearms to chest level as the power of the Holy Spirit rises in her. Faith's power bursts from the inside out, and she's ingulfed in fire. With all her might, she explodes straight through the blockade and slams through the roof.

Faith slams into her body. Light flashes everywhere. Frank and Hezekiah jump back. Faith's body levitates from the table. Murder and the other demons fly in to kill them. Faith's power explodes with light, incinerating Murder and the evil spirits. Murder screams as he and the rest of the evil spirits burn away under the power of the Holy Spirit.

The light fades, and Faith stands up, fully awake. She stares at Hezekiah, and he gazes into her eyes and gasps. His jaw drops, and his tears of sadness turn to joy.

"My God," Frank says above a whisper.

Tears streaming down Hezekiah's face, he moves in, hugs her, and lifts her off her feet. Frank stares, tears of joy streaming down his face, watching the happy scene.

Chapter 54

THE REUNION

FOR THE NEXT FEW HOURS, HEZEKIAH AND FRANK celebrate and thank God that He brought Faith back from the dead. They go to all of Faith's favorite places in town. Money and time are no object as they thank God for allowing her to come back. She can hardly get a word in as they take her to many places throughout the city. Afterward, Frank lets the happy couple go home.

Hezekiah and Faith are at their home on the patio, sitting down on lawn chairs. Hezekiah silently watches his bride with a smile on his face and tears in his eyes.

"What is it, baby?" asks Faith.

"I thought I lost you," Hezekiah says with a dry mouth.

Faith goes over to him, sits on his lap, and puts her arms around him. She kisses him on the cheek, and warmth travels across his face.

"What did you see while you were in heaven? And how did you come down the way you did?" asks Hezekiah.

"I don't remember much about what I saw, but I did see Jesus, my mother, and the twelve apostles."

"Really?"

"Yeah," says Faith as she turns her head to stare off into the distance.

"There is something you're not telling me," he says.

"Do you remember your first battle in the City of Light?" asks Faith.

"Yeah. I fought against a demonic tiger creature. What about it?"

"Well, I have something I have to tell you."

"What is it?"

"I'd rather show you than tell you."

Faith gets up from his lap and stands in the middle of the patio. Hezekiah turns his chair and sits on the edge of his seat. He looks at her quietly. Faith smiles at him.

"You ready?" she says.

Hezekiah nods. Faith shoots her arm into the air to summon the sword of the Spirit.

ABOUT THE AUTHOR

WAYMAN JACKSON IS A CHRISTIAN WRITER WITH a focus on reaching people for Christ. Accepting a relationship with Jesus as a teenager, he wanted others to experience freedom from guilt and shame. He always had an active imagination that ran wild if left unchecked. Armed with creative vision, and a desire to save the lost, he sets out to write novels to draw people to Jesus. Interested in a good story, once he has an idea, he will naturally analyze it all the way through and commit to it until its completion. Stay tuned for more titles in the Sword of the Spirit series.

SCRIPTURE REFERENCE PAGE

MANY TIMES, IN THE BOOK, THE CHARACTERS share specific Scripture or reference them. Gathered here is the exact wording of these passages. I hope you will use them for your own research and spiritual growth.

Luke 6:45 Berean Study Bible
The good man brings good things out of the good treasure of his heart, and the evil man brings evil things out of the evil treasure of his heart. For out of the overflow of the heart, the mouth speaks.

Revelation 3:7-8 NIV:
"To the angel of the church in Philadelphia write:
These are the words of him who is holy and true, who holds the key of David. What he opens no one can shut, and what he shuts no one can open. I know your deeds. See, I have placed before you an open door that no one can shut. I know that you have little strength, yet you have kept my word and have not denied my name.

Psalm 91:1 NIV
Whoever dwells in the shelter of the Most High will rest in the shadow of the Almighty.

Joshua 1:9 NIV
Be strong and courageous. Do not be afraid; do not be discouraged, for the Lord your God will be with you wherever you go.

Matthew 26:26-28 NIV
While they were eating, Jesus took bread, and when he had given thanks, he broke it and gave it to his disciples, saying, "Take and eat; this is my body." Then he took a cup, and when he had given thanks, he gave it to them, saying, "Drink from it, all of you. This is my blood of the covenant, which is poured out for many for the forgiveness of sins.

Song of Songs 1:1-4 NIV
Let him kiss me with the kisses of his mouth—
for your love is more delightful than wine.
Pleasing is the fragrance of your perfumes;
your name is like perfume poured out.
No wonder the young women love you!
Take me away with you—let us hurry!
Let the king bring me into his chambers.

Song of Songs 2:14 NIV
My dove in the clefts of the rock,
in the hiding places on the mountainside,
show me your face,
let me hear your voice;
for your voice is sweet,
and your face is lovely.

2 Chronicles 7:13-14 NIV
When I shut up the heavens so that there is no rain, or command locusts to devour the land or send a plague among my people, if my people, who are called by my name, will humble themselves and pray

and seek my face and turn from their wicked ways, then I will hear from heaven, and I will forgive their sin and will heal their land.

Numbers 22:23 NIV
When the donkey saw the angel of the LORD standing in the road with a drawn sword in his hand, it turned off the road into a field. Balaam beat it to get it back on the road.

James 5:14-16 NIV
Is anyone among you sick? Let them call the elders of the church to pray over them and anoint them with oil in the name of the Lord. And the prayer offered in faith will make the sick person well; the Lord will raise them up. If they have sinned, they will be forgiven. Therefore confess your sins to each other and pray for each other so that you may be healed. The prayer of a righteous person is powerful and effective.

Romans:10-9-13NIV
If you declare with your mouth, "Jesus is Lord," and believe in your heart that God raised him from the dead, you will be saved. For it is with your heart that you believe and are justified, and it is with your mouth that you profess your faith and are saved. As Scripture says, "Anyone who believes in him will never be put to shame." For there is no difference between Jew and Gentile—the same Lord is Lord of all and richly blesses all who call on him, for, "Everyone who calls on the name of the Lord will be saved."

Psalm 27:1 NIV
The LORD is my light and my salvation—
whom shall I fear?
The LORD is the stronghold of my life—
of whom shall I be afraid?"

CPSIA information can be obtained
at www.ICGtesting.com
Printed in the USA
LVHW051332261221
707005LV00004B/82

9 781662 835148